When Are You Going to Do As You're Told?

Ray Speakman

authorHOUSE®

AuthorHouse™ UK
1663 Liberty Drive
Bloomington, IN 47403 USA
www.authorhouse.co.uk
Phone: 0800.197.4150

Published by AuthorHouse 11/28/2014

ISBN: 978-1-4969-9724-1 (sc)
ISBN: 978-1-4969-9727-2 (e)

Contents

Dedication

For Matilda, Violet, William and Oliver.

1.

Kick the Can

It wasn't summer anymore, but we refused to believe it was over. In my back garden, squeezing the last minutes of light out of the day, were Arthur, Victor and me. Eric wasn't there. His mother wouldn't let him play out if darkness was a possibility.

We were playing a variation on hide-and-seek called 'kick the can'. One person was 'on' and hung about by an old tin can which used to hold beans or peas or something, while the others ran off to hide. If you could sneak back and kick the can while the person who was 'on' was searching, you won and you escaped being 'on' the next time around.

Darkness soaked into the corners of the garden. Perfect for hiding. I knew the best places, the deep inaccessible places, the places where I could wrap the darkness around me like an invisibility cloak. I squeezed myself into the hedge at the bottom of the garden and then pushed myself up through its branches so that I was two feet or so off the ground. Then I was still. I could smell the earth beneath and feel the leaves like a second skin around me. The hedge had absorbed me.

Arthur was 'on' and I could hear him as he tried to bluff us into coming out by saying he could see where we were. I didn't know where Victor was and neither Victor nor Arthur would have any idea where I was. I wanted to laugh out loud imagining their puzzlement and how it would quickly turn to panic as they wondered what had become of me.

I was so enclosed, so warm, so *outside* of everything I felt I could sleep there. No one would ever find me and I would be like an observer, an invisible watcher, a ghost in the shadows seeing but not seen. The darkness wasn't frightening because I could see through it and I could control it. It wasn't a mystery. I was the mystery.

Time went. The shadows had now stained everything so completely that almost all of the garden's detail had gone. I couldn't hear Arthur or Victor. The can hadn't been kicked. I hadn't been found. I waited.

Those feelings of being in charge, of wanting to laugh because I was winning, of looking down on everyone, were slowly ebbing away. The worst thing that *could* happen during a game of kick-the-can or hide-and-seek *had* happened. I hadn't been found - I had been forgotten! Life had moved on without me in it. Arthur and Victor had simply lost interest and wandered off home and I was still here, in the darkness, alone and trapped in a hedge!

The darkness that had been so comfortable, that had been *my* darkness, my ally, now filled itself with shapes and half heard noises that were beyond anything I could recognise or understand. And the hedge didn't seem to want to let me go. I had entangled myself in it so completely and now I had forgotten the way back out. Branches poked at me whichever way I squirmed, leaves blocked my vision whichever way I looked and the earth below my legs seemed to have receded so that instead of getting closer to the ground I felt as if I was moving higher and higher until......the hedge seemed to give up, get bored with me, become so irritated by my childish panic it just opened its arms and let me fall out.

Silence. No sound or sign of Arthur and Victor. No lights on in the house either. Perhaps I'd fallen through the hedge into another time zone? A parallel universe with no friends or family.

"Arthur? Victor? I give in. You can come out now."

I was certain they were somewhere in the garden. I felt sure I could half hear them – breathing, watching. No answer. Nothing. I didn't want to look behind me. Something told me not to turn around and look into the hedge.

The world had changed, the light had almost gone, I focused on our house, my bedroom window, and the kitchen window – and the man! There was a man standing in our kitchen! A very tall still man with a pale, round face. Worse still, I was certain he was watching me.

My stomach turned over, and then it turned over again and again. It wouldn't stop turning over. I stared at the man. He stared at me. I couldn't move. He didn't move. I couldn't think. My brain just made this screaming noise like a radio that can't find any stations. No thoughts, just static.

And through all this, behind all this, a high pitched ring, repeating over and over and making absolutely no sense.

****

2.

Who was that on the phone?

A light came on. Then another. Then another.

"Jimmy? Jimmy?"

The kitchen light was turned on and I saw my mother through the window. The man was still there but it wasn't a man. It was my mum's white straw garden hat hanging on the wall on a peg with some sort of jacket hanging below it and the top of a pair of wellies just showing below.

"Jimmy? Jimmy?"

I ran up the garden and in through the back door.

"Who was that on the phone?"

"I was in the garden."

"It's pitch black dark!"

"We were playing out."

"We?"

"Arthur and Victor. They've just gone home."

"So you thought you'd cut the hedge, did you?

"What?"

"You've got privet hedge all over yourself. How many times have I told you to listen for the phone?"

On this occasion I hadn't actually ignored the telephone. I was too busy being terrified by the feeling that there was someone in the hedge behind me and then seeing that face in the kitchen window. Mind you I usually did ignore the telephone. For one reason it probably *wasn't* for me and for another reason, it *might* have been for me. If it was *not* for me it was probably someone asking for my dad to do a painting and decorating job; if it *was* for me it was almost certainly someone I did not want to speak to – but more of that later. Either way she was right. I usually just sat there on the sofa, or sprawled there as my mother would say, reading my book hoping the ringing would stop.

She dropped her shopping, sighed and dialled that number you dial to find out if you've had any calls then pressed the button to put the phone on speaker. "You were called at seven sixteen today by…." She wrote the number down, turned the phone off and then just stood there. "What time is it now?"

"Er…"

"It's nineteen minutes past seven! The phone rang three minutes ago. And whose number is that anyway? It could be anyone wanting a decorating job doing. It could be a massive well paid job for all you know. How could you not hear it? And sit up on that sofa. I'm fed up with you sprawling on that sofa and not answering the phone. When are you going to do as you're told? You know very well how important phone calls are. When are you going to make a contribution to this family? How many times do I have to tell you? It could be hundreds of pounds coming in for us."

"I was reading."

"You're always reading. Who's going to buy you books if your dad doesn't get any work?"

"I could go to the library."

"The library? You've got a hell of a cheek, you have! Threatening me with the library! I'm going to go down to that school about you and your lip. Mr Nixon would be very interested to hear about the way you sprawl everywhere. Your dad and I are working all the hours and all you can do is sprawl on the sofa, come up with smarty answers and ignore the phone!"

"I do answer the phone. I've answered it a hell of a lot of times."

"What did you just say? What was that word you just used?"

"What word?"

"You know what word!"

"You swore first. You said, 'Hell of a lot of times'."

"No I didn't! Where do you get words like that from? You don't hear them in this house. I know you think you hear them, but you definitely don't hear them here. It's all in your head – or - it's those so-called weird friends of yours! Eric and Arthur whatever they're called. And that girl who thinks she's a boy – Victor something. I bet they're sprawled out in their houses now, swearing and not answering the phone. I'm going to stop you going out."

"Before you go down to the school about me, or after?"

"Right, that's it. Get to bed!"

"It's only half past seven at night!"

"I don't care. Get to bed."

"I was only joking. You don't have to go all hypersensitive."

"And that's another thing."

"What?"

"Swearing AND using big words. When did you ever hear your dad or me showing off with big words? Get to bed. Now. We'll see about 'hypersensitive' when I tell your dad about all this."

Half way up the stairs the phone rang.

"Answer that phone!"

"I've been sent to bed."

"Do you want me to put that book in the bin?"

I came back into the living room, picked up the pencil by the phone and very deliberately made ready to write down whatever message I was about to receive from the caller. My mother folded her arms and nodded with just the faintest hint of satisfaction.

"The McConkey House. How may I help you?"

"Is that you, McConkey? Or your butler?" This was followed by a loud jeering laugh.

You know I said earlier that I did not answer the phone because it was probably for my parents, but that I also didn't like to answer the phone in case it *was* for me? The second reason for not wanting to answer was now on the other end of the phone. Laughing.

"It's for me, Mum."

"Who is it?"

"Henley Phipps."

"Ahhh! Is he out of hospital?"

"Is that your mum, McConkey? Put me on speaker. Hello, Mrs McConkey. It's Henley," he said – making his voice go high and trying to sound all sweet.

"Are you out of hospital, Henley?"

"Yes, Mrs McConkey. Thank you. I've just come out but I'm not allowed to play out so I wondered if your Jimmy could come round and – see me – and lend me one of his books or something."

"Of course he could, Henley, love. Can he come on Saturday morning?"

I was waving my arms about, shaking my head violently and mouthing, "No, no, no!"

"That would be great, Mrs McConkey. I'll tell my mum to expect him. Thank you. Bye, bye, bye, bye, bye...."

"Mum!! How can I go and see him? He's had half his face cut off? He'll be grotesque. How can I look at him?"

"He hasn't had half his face off! He's just got a little scar behind his ear. His mother told me."

"And all down his neck and over his head. Have you actually seen him?"

"No, but his mother said…"

"Then how can you condemn me to actually being in the same room with a great big red scar. I'll have to look at him. He'll talk me and I'll have to answer."

"Since when have you been short of an answer? Look, Jimmy, just take him a few books…"

"He can't read. Everybody knows that."

"Then it's a shame, isn't it? You should be feeling sorry for him, then. You could help him learn."

"What? To read? The teachers have been trying for years!"

"Not just that. You could help him learn to adjust to seeing people after his operation. All you have to do is just be normal. Don't stare at his head."

"Mum! I won't be able to even look at his head!"

As I headed up to bed my mother called me back. "Who did you say was here before?"

"Arthur and Eric."

"Then who's that kid down at the bottom of the garden?"

My stomach started turning over again. I ran into my bedroom and, without turning the light on, looked out of the window. No one.

"I can't see a kid. There wasn't anyone else. Just us."

There was a pause. My mother obviously went to the back kitchen window. "I'm sure I saw someone. A kid with white hair and a round face."

****

3.

Victor

The only way to cope with seeing Henley Phipps was to round up the lost names gang and get them to come with me. We called ourselves that because we all had first names that time had forgotten: Eric, Arthur and Victor, who was a girl but one of us anyway. My first name was Jim and my second name McConkey. Time hadn't forgotten my first name, but I wished it had forgotten my second name. Despite my declared aversion to the telephone the only thing to do was to call each of them and get them to meet me at the Lime Avenue shops near where Henley Phipps lived.

Just as I was about to dial Eric's number I looked down and saw it. Eric's number on the pad next to the phone.

"Mum? What's this telephone number on the pad?"

My mother came to the top of the stairs with her arms full of bedding. "I'm changing the bed!"

"At this time of night?"

"What other time do I get?"

"What's this number here on the pad?"

"It's the number you didn't answer when I was coming in."

"Oh no! Its Eric's number. Eric must have phoned me."

"That'll teach you to do what you're told and answer the phone then, won't it?"

"What do you think he wanted?"

"To have a swear at you, I should think, for not answering the phone."

Eric's phone rang for ages. Then his mother answered.

"No, love. He's not going to be in on Saturday. He's going out with his granddad and his friend, Arthur. They're going to the Science museum in town, to look at the steam engines. Is it Jimmy?"

"Is Victor going?"

"No, I'm sure she isn't. Eric tried to phone both of you but got no answer from you and Victor had to wait in for the vegetable man's van, so they've just nipped around to his granddad's to make the arrangements. This is Jimmy I'm talking to, isn't it?"

I hated being called Jimmy. "Yes. Jim. It's me." I don't know if I was upset or just frustrated but I got that funny feeling you get behind your nose when you're about to cry and my eyes started prickling with water.

"What a shame you missed the call. They won't be back until nine. They promised me nine. What a shame!"

She knew. She just knew! I hate it when people hear a little catch in your voice so say, 'what a shame' over and over. I think they do it so that they can watch you trying to stop yourself from crying. Then they say, "Have I upset you?" And when you say, "No!" because if you tried to say a whole sentence you would start bawling uncontrollably so you just cough, and they say, "Never mind, love. Never mind," – which makes it worse.

I said goodbye to Eric's mum as politely as I could and dialled Victor's number. Thank goodness for Victor. Thank goodness she was in. Thank goodness she answered the phone.

"Hey, Victor? Is that you?"

"Jim?"

"Do you want to meet up by the Lime Avenue shops on Saturday morning?"

"Okay. Eric and Arthur are looking at steam engines."

"I know. Eric's mum told me on the phone."

"You answered the phone?"

"Funny! No, he phoned me earlier and I just phoned him back. His mum said they were round at his granddad's making arrangements. Why aren't you going?"

"Didn't fancy it. Since Eric discovered steam engines and railways he seems to have developed a one track mind." Pause. "That was a joke – railways – train lines – one track!"

I laughed – belatedly. Eric used to go on all the time about heavy goods vehicles, even to the point of pretending to be one around the playground at playtime. Turning a massive imaginary steering wheel and making beeping noises to show that he was reversing. He had red hair that was too big for his head. Arthur on the other hand, who tended to believe everything he was told and had a smile that was too big for his face, once had a thing about the Lewis Carroll 'Jabberwocky' poem. I had noticed that as Eric and Arthur spent more time together, and a little less time with Victor and me, their interests were also coinciding. Trains: in museums, in books, in poems, in pictures, in stories, on the internet. Which quite a lot of the time, just left Victor and me.

Although Victor was a girl (really called Victoria only you wouldn't dare call her that) and I was a boy, people did not roll their eyes at us and say, "Oh yeah. I see. You and Victor. I get it!" Either they just didn't see us as different or they would not take the risk of seeing us, or saying that they saw us, as different. We wouldn't hit them or anything, but Victor had this withering way with words that would leave you shrunken and speechless.

"So what do you want to do instead?" said Victor.

"I thought we might call in on Henley Phipps and cheer him up."

"What?"

"I thought we might call on Henley..."

"I heard you the first time. I just didn't believe you really said it. You hate Henley Phipps, more to the point he hates you. He can't stop hating you. He can't live without hating you!"

She was right. I didn't really know why I was suggesting visiting Henley Phipps, except my mother wanted me to. She felt sorry for him after his life-threatening operation but, more than that, felt sorry for his mother – who must lay awake all night wondering why she had a son who everybody was scared of. She probably thought people kept their distance because of his scars, not because he was a bully and a sneerer and as hard as nails.

Victor sensed my confusion so came up with something that she felt sure would tip the argument in favour of *not* going to visit Henley Phipps. "We'd have to see his operation scar."

"So?"

She knew this was either avoiding the issue or bravado and she knew I couldn't do bravado so she pressed on with the thought. "We'd have to look at his head, Jim. I'm okay with that, but you...!"

"My mum says he keeps his curtains closed most of the time. It'll be dark."

"Dark? That's even worse! If you can't see his scars, you'll end up imagining them! You know what your imagination is like?"

I didn't rise to the bait. I knew what she would say if I asked her what my imagination was like. She's say words like 'lurid' or "sensational' or 'livid' or 'shocking'. Victor liked lists. When she did a piece of writing at school she would put in at least two adjectives for every noun, or two adverbs to every verb. She had a brain like a game of Scrabble, full of double and triple words scores. You didn't stand a chance.

"Just be there on Saturday at about ten. Bring a book for him to read."

"Read?"

"Oh yeah, Victor, that reminds me. Talking about the dark and people with over-the-top imaginations, where did you and Arthur go last night? I thought we were supposed to be playing kick-the-can?"

"Where did *we* go? Where did you go? It was you who cleared off and left *us*! You were gone for hours so we went home before it got completely dark."

"I could have been lying fatally injured in the shadows, the life blood leaking …. What's a good word for the way the blood leaks and won't stop?"

"Bleeding."

"No – there's a long word – in-something. Like unstoppable. And it was so dark. Have you noticed how there are two sorts of dark? There's the dark that hides things and you don't know what they are so you mostly think they are going to be really scary things. So scary that you can't even imagine what they might be."

"Yeah, I know that sort of dark, said Victor enthusiastically. "So scary that if whatever it might be is behind you or under something or round the corner, you daren't even look. I know that sort. It makes you, like, freeze! What's the other sort of dark?"

"Where there's nothing. Empty. No sounds or thoughts. Just blank."

"Which sort was it last night?" Victor was really interested now.

"The first sort. It was like my eyes were gradually switching off like on a dimmer switch and my ears were being turned up, like a volume control. I was certain there was somebody in the garden. 'Course I thought at first it was you two, hiding from me, but when it wasn't I had this thing where my stomach turned into a washing machine on full spin and the inside of my brain was trying to find a way out and my whole body was just seized up on the spot."

"See what I mean about your imagination?"

"This is real, Victor. I was trapped in the hedge and there was this great big bloke with a round face standing in the kitchen. I couldn't escape. Then the phone rang and my mum came in and called me so I ran up the garden –"

"More scared of your mum than the great big bloke with the round face…."

"And realised that the bloke with the round face was my mother's gardening hat hanging on a peg."

"Imagination then?"

"Not really because later on my mother said who was that kid with the white hair down the garden?"

"What kid?"

"Exactly. When I was trapped in the hedge I just knew that something was there. In the dark."

"That explains it then. See you at the Lime Avenue shops, ten o'clock, Saturday morning. Come on your own. Don't bring any kids with white hair."

"Okay then."

"Hang on. Are you still there, Jim?

"Yeah."

"Inexorably. That word you wanted that means unstoppable. When you said you could have been dead in the hedge with the life blood leaking out of you ..."

"Inexorably? No that can't be it. Doesn't that mean like something really gross. Disgusting. Like dog poo?"

Victor sighed. "No – it definitely means unstoppable. Look it up."

****

4.

Unstoppable

Some days you wake up with an inexorable feeling of dread. At first you don't know what it is exactly that you are dreading, you just feel this gloom sitting in your chest. Today it was something about Saturday morning. This didn't make sense for a few seconds because Saturday should be the absolute ungloomiest day of the week; no homework you've forgotten to do, no surprise tests at school, no chance of being ambushed on the way to...... oh NO!! Henley Phipps! He wasn't going to be lying in wait for me somewhere between home and school because I was actually going to see him in his house! Today! Saturday morning. How come I agreed to that?

Monday to Saturday my mum worked in the morning at the Lime Avenue optician's and in the afternoon during the week she did a couple of hours at my school in the kitchens. I think she quite liked the optician's job but found the kitchen job a bit of a bind. She only did it while my dad was trying to establish himself as a painter and decorator – hence all that fuss about answering the phone. So today, she just had the optician's job; as a result breakfast felt a bit less rushed than usual. Cereal and toast was replaced by poached egg on toast, and we all sat down at the table instead of standing or pacing around the kitchen with food in our hands.

After my mum and dad had discussed the work he was doing today and what time he planned to finish, they turned to me. They were all smiles! Mum had obviously told my dad about my saintly plan to visit the sick and traumatised Henley Phipps, how most kids would be scared to make such a visit and how proud they were of their brave and selfless son.

Perhaps I had been too 'shut up and bear it' in the past. Maybe I hadn't said often enough about the bullying and the general scariness. I was sure I had! Sometimes it's not that parents don't listen, it's perhaps that they don't want to *hear*. When everything is going okay at school and with other kids, they look for problems and think you're hiding something. Then when you really are worried, or stressed, or unhappy, they think you are definitely making it up or imagining things.

Anyway, my mum knew quite a lot of detail about Henley Phipps' operation because it was the optician where she worked that first spotted that Henley might have something seriously wrong with him. I could have told her years ago that he had something seriously wrong with him: he was a complete menace to society! Then that wasn't what the optician had spotted. He was fairly certain that Henley had a blood clot just behind one of his eyes and pressing on the optic nerve.

Hence the big operation – and the scars – and everyone feeling sorry for him – and trying to talk about him in a sympathetic way.

So just for once I left our house in Pineapple Road (how embarrassing it that for a place to live?) in my mum and dad's good books. No warnings or advice offered, no talk about coming home time, no doubts about who I would be meeting on the way or afterwards.

I had arranged to meet Victor by the Lime Avenue shops. The whole estate had street names after fruit and vegetables. Consequently it was known as the 'five a day' estate. Our road was Pineapple Road, then there was Lime Avenue, Russet Close (where the school was), Walnut Avenue, Bramley Gardens, Artichoke Drive, and Cherry Lane and so on and so on.

I used to wonder who had done all this, who it was who thought up street names to embarrass kids with when they had to give their address for the register at the beginning of the school year. I imagined someone who fancied himself as a stand-up comedian, sitting in an office eating sausage rolls and drinking tea and dreaming up 'hilarious' street names and then squirting out crumbs as he laughed at his own funniness. Then maybe again, he just got his computer to do it while he dozed in his chair. I wonder what job they gave him once all the streets were named. Perhaps he had to move to another estate somewhere else in the country where his thinking up daft names experience would come in handy, especially if the authorities wanted people they sent to live there feel stupid.

Lime Avenue shops were at the centre of the estate. They were quite grand, built in a sort of crescent with a slip road taking you past each shop, parking spaces and a great big grass area between the shops and Lime Avenue proper. My mum said that when they first moved here these were actual shops – all of them: butchers', green grocers', grocers', sewing shop, newsagents', chippy, and hardware shop - everything. Now there was a mini-supermarket, a couple of charity shops, a café, a real ale off licence and the rest were offices for estate agents, accountants and of course, the optician's.

The chippy was the sole survivor of Lime Avenue Shops as they were first imagined. The chippy was like the

Stonehenge of the five-a-day estate, a mysterious relic of long forgotten times.

It was actually quite good to walk towards the shops without being afraid that Henley Phipps would leap out of a gateway and accuse me of something. A funny thing had happened though, since his operation. I avoided walking past his gate, not because I thought he might suddenly appear, I knew that wouldn't happen, it was because I knew he was in his house, with the curtains drawn, being ill. Lying there groaning and thinking about what he wrote in that letter he wrote to me from the hospital, 'Just you wait, McConkey!'

Or maybe it was because I thought his mother might come running out appealing to me to come and see her bed-bound son. Or perhaps she would accuse me – this was the worst – of being a hypocrite, pretending to do nice things for her son but really hating him and hoping his operation would go badly and he would have to go into a special home for kids with terrible faces miles from anywhere, especially here.

I waited for Victor outside the estate agents looking at the houses for sale or rent in Hazel Grove, Chestnut Gardens and Satsuma Street, wondering if that thinker-up of place names was at all embarrassed now by what he had done.

Satsuma Street! Sick and wrong! And Walnut Avenue! Where all the nutters lived! Talking of nutters, Chucky Lockett lived in Walnut Avenue – remind me to tell you about him later.

Victor appeared on the other side of the grass bordering the shops. She was frowning.

"Are you sure about this, Jim?"

"No, but I promised my mum."

"Promises can be broken." Victor saw me hesitate and so pressed on. "You might faint when you see his scars. The sight of him might set you off on bad dreams for years and years. He might be all pathetic and start you off feeling guilty about how much you've hated him. Or he might be worse, all aggressive and loud and impossible to answer."

"True."

"Which bit?"

"Take your pick."

"So, shall we go somewhere else?" said Victor turning away and leaning forward like you do at the beginning of a race and someone has shouted, 'get set'.

"No. It's not just me. Everyone hates Henley Phipps and the more everyone hates him the more hateful he gets. His hatefulness is inexorable."

"That's my word. You said you thought it meant dog poo. So why does his inexorable hatefulness make us have to go and see him?"

"No idea. Come on," I said and we headed towards Henley's house.

****

5.

The Darkness

"Oh, he'll be so pleased you've come. He's stuck in the house all day. In his bedroom. Go up, go on. He still likes to have his curtains closed but you soon get used to the dark." She shouted up the stairs, "Henley, your friends are coming up now!"

His bedroom door was slightly ajar. We peeped through and could just about see in the thin splinter of light from the window half of Henley's head. He was motionless. In the dark.

I half whispered to Victor, "He's dead! He's definitely dead! Look, Victor. I don't want to see him if he's dead. Definitely. I've never seen anyone dead."

"You've already seen him!" She eased me to one side and had a look. "I think you're right. He's gone all – that thing that bodies do when they're dead where they go all rigid – like when you see a dead cat in the road – all stiff and frozen."

"I never look. Do you think we ought to tell his mum he's dead?

"She might cry," Victor said with a look of disgust on her face. "I never know what to do when people cry."

Victor thought for a minute so I said, "Perhaps we could just make a run for it?"

"Then she'd think we'd killed him!"

"Do you want to see my drawings?" said Henley.

My stomach turned into a solid block of ice and I could just about see Victor's ET eyes getting bigger and bigger. I'm not sure if we were relieved or disappointed that he was alive, but still very, very scared, we stepped tentatively into the room. It was so dark in there it took a minute or so to work out what was what, exactly where the bed was and exactly where Henley's voice was coming from.

Then we saw him, or at least we saw his silhouette, just about. He was sitting cross legged on his bed holding out a pile of drawing paper. Once the door had closed behind us we could see even less of his head than we had from the landing. He was deep in the shadows.

"We can't really see any drawings, Henley. It's too dark."

"They're pictures to go with the words."

"The words?" I would have looked at Victor but my eyes weren't used to the darkness.

"Agonising. Excruciating. Tormenting. Burning. Harrowing. Searing."

There was silence.

"And these are the pictures to go with the words."

"Fantastic words, Henley," said Victor.

"They used to come up to me and say, 'On a scale of one to ten, what mark would you give the pain today?' Two or three out of ten for a bit of an ache or a tingle. Eight or nine out of ten for – one of these words: excruciating, searing or whatever. I think they liked thinking up the words, the nurses and doctors. I used to ask them to write them down, and then I'd do a drawing to go with the word."

We were becoming more accustomed to the lack of light in the room and so could make out more of the drawings. Faces, scrunched up faces; the higher the number out of ten, the scrunchier the face.

"What word did you have for ten out of ten?"

He pulled out a sheet of paper and held it up. No word. The face was only vaguely there, a shadow behind a huge tangle of black scribbles, like an out of control ball of wire wool.

"Searing is a good word, Henley," said Victor, referring to one of the less scribbly drawings.

"Yeah, I like that word, too," said Henley.

Victor said, "And was it – you know – the operation – was it painful like all those words?"

"Not really; I don't feel pain, me. Anyway, I didn't care."

I could see what Victor was doing. She was moving into social worker mode to get on the right side of him. We were both pretty scared of him actually. Not the scar. Him. Henley could be very violent even without surgery.

Immune to reason, he was, at the best of times. Not that times were ever at their best where he was involved.

"On a scale of one to ten, Henley, how *harrowing* was the whole experience?"

"You nicked that word from me!"

"I *learned* it from you, Henley. It's an absolutely fantastic word. Evocative."

"That's not one of my words, no. I never had no evocative pain that I know of anyway."

Victor tried not to look at me.

"You learned a new word from me?" said Henley, a bit pathetically I thought.

"Quite a few words, actually", I chipped in.

"Sound," - at which point he leaned forward into a small bar of light slanting through his bedroom window. At first his face looked quite normal. He was side-on to us facing out of the window. Then he turned to look the other way to gather up his drawings and we saw. He was like something in a story. One side of him unchanged, the other side of his head – hair shaved off and a red line going from his temple, up over his ear, down the other side and on towards his shirt collar. I made myself not gasp and I think Victor did the same.

Henley Phipps now looked as frightening as we always thought he was. It was as though his hatefulness had burst out of him for everyone to see.

"They said my hair will grow again," he said as though he knew what we were thinking, "and if I let it grow quite long the scar will disappear underneath. No one will notice."

"Will it take long?" I said and then held my breath in case I'd said the wrong thing.

"My mum says I can stay off school until it's grown. I could go fishing. You could come with me if you wanted. You could be my crew at Crowton Mill Pond."

"We can't stay off school," Victor said.

"No. On the weekends and holidays. We could go on our bikes and you could carry all my stuff and watch me catch pike or even carp. There are carp in Crowton

Mill Pond you know, whatever anyone says. Great big fat carp. I'd have my picture in the newspaper."

We didn't know what to say. Carp? Can you eat them? Why would you want to catch them? And would someone really want to take a photograph of Henley?

"And while we're catching carp, we could watch out for that kid and catch him." Henley said this almost casually – as though it was not all that important, but I'm sure he knew it would catch our attention.

"There's a kid in the pond?"

We waited for him to say more. Victor's ET eyes had gone so big I could see them through the darkness. The silence satisfied Henley that he had captured our interest so he went on.

"Not *in* the pond," he said nonchalantly, "near it somewhere. And I don't think it's actually a kid. It's like a kid zombie. I've heard he escapes sometimes from wherever he lives – in a grave probably – and hangs around the estate. Have you lot seen him – he's got all white hair and a really round face? And no eyes."

"No," I said. "No. White hair?"

Victor looked at me with that look on her face that said, "Why are you lying?" but she said nothing.

So we sat there in a dark bedroom saying nothing but all of us thinking, probably, about these two kids. One hiding in his bedroom because he didn't want anyone to see his scars and the other hiding somewhere near a pond for who knows what reason. It couldn't be because he had a round face and white hair – and he must have had eyes, else how did he get in our back garden? It didn't make sense. Was Henley right? Was this kid really a zombie? And if he was a zombie what was he doing in our back garden when we were playing kick-the-can? *If* he was in our back garden. Maybe my Mum just caught a passing glimpse of her own reflection in the window pane and thought it was someone out there. And what was he doing at Crowton Mill Pond? It was about a mile away, surrounded by woods and down a long muddy track.

"Anyway," went on Henley eventually, "we can't have zombies living round here."

"They might frighten the carp," I said and knew it was the wrong thing to say before I'd closed my mouth.

"It's nothing to try and be funny about, Jimmy McConkey. People who try to be funny about serious things get their heads bashed in! Zombies are just not right. Everybody knows that. They shouldn't be allowed. They don't look right and they're not from round here. They don't fit in. They can't talk and they eat people's faces off. Something has to be done."

Victor couldn't keep quiet. "They don't exist, Henley."

"That's what *they* want you to think."

"Who – the zombies?"

"No, them on the telly and the newspapers. Them in charge on the council and that. They don't want us to know about the zombies, do they? It's obvious. If we knew there were zombies we'd be running round screaming and going crackers. The schools would have to close."

We said nothing. What could we say? He really believed all this. Schools closing might be an idea worth exploring though!

"I think we ought to get a gang of us, go up there and sort him out. Super heroes!!" and he punched the air.

"You and your mates could come fishing with me and while we're there, disguised as innocent anglers, we could lay in wait and when the zombie appears we can sort him out."

"What does that mean, sort him out?" said Victor.

"It means – sort – him – out. Yes!" and he punched the air again, with both hands this time, like a boxer having a mad go at a punch bag. "He wouldn't stand a chance.

He'd be dead frightened of us. I could bring Chucky Lockett – he likes fighting."

He would be dead frightened of you, Henley, I thought. He definitely would not want to take a bite out of your face – or Chucky Lockett's.

"So what do you think? Tomorrow? Sunday? Or next weekend? I could ask Chucky Lockett if he wanted to come. He's strong."

Chucky Lockett was this older kid who lived down Walnut Avenue – remember, I mentioned Walnut Avenue earlier – where the nutters live. Not in every house, obviously, but in quite a few. Chucky Lockett was really big. I think he did body building or ate a lot, I'm not sure, but it left him with huge arms and shoulders and a head like a pea. I definitely didn't want him with Eric, Arthur, Victor and me. He was another one of those kids, like Henley, who was always on the look-out for an insult so he could take offence. I'd rather have a zombie for a mate!

"Not tomorrow, Henley, no. We'd have to ask our parents anyway."

"Okay. Great! That will give my hair more time to grow. And I tell you what, if you come I'll let you have the big metal notice I found in the bushes by the mill pond. It's fantastic. It says, BEWARE OF THE TRAINS. *By order"*

"What trains?"

As we left, Henley's mum gave us a biscuit each.

****

6.

Beware of the Trains and Zombies

"Did you actually see the 'BEWARE OF THE TRAINS *By order'* notice?" This was Arthur in school on Monday morning. "Because if you didn't actually see it, Henley Phipps might have made it up."

"Henley Phipps can't make things up. His brain wouldn't cope," said Eric.

"And the logic of that is that if he's telling the truth about the railway notice he must be telling the truth about the zombie," offered Victor, "which makes all of it a bit hard to believe."

We all nodded thoughtfully. The idea that there might be railway remains somewhere nearby was planted in Eric's mind and you could tell by the way he was wriggling and gasping that he might explode any minute. He was always looking at pictures of various railway notices and suchlike on the internet. "But – but – he could be telling the truth about the railway notice and lying about the zombie – or imagining it."

"He couldn't do that either. He lives in an imagination-free zone," said Victor. "Slow down, Eric, you're going to start hyperventilating if you go on like this."

"I'd really love to see that notice. I'd love to own it, wouldn't you? I'd stick it up on our front gate or – or – on my bedroom wall! Couldn't we just give in and go fishing with him just once so that he'd hand over the notice?"

"What about the zombie?' said Arthur, his eyes seeming to expand as he imagined what we might have to face.

Victor laughed. "What about the zombie?" she said. "What zombie?"

Arthur was still unsure, "Honestly, say honestly that there is no zombie at Crowton Mill."

"If there is no zombie at Crowton Mill," said Eric, "why, from what you said, does Phipps want us all to go up there like a mob and sort him, or it, out. What does that mean exactly? Sort him out. I hope he doesn't mean fighting. I would do fishing as long as I didn't catch anything, but I definitely don't want to do any fighting – with zombies or anybody else. I'm just interested in trains, railway lines, bridges, stations, signals, signal boxes and the railway people. And notices. I'd really love to find a notice that said that anyone found trespassing on this railway shall on conviction be liable to a penalty not exceeding forty shillings. I saw a photo of one like that on the internet. I would love to actually own a notice like that. When I was out or in school I could think about it and look forward to seeing it when I came in."

"How much is that? Forty shillings?" said Arthur whose interest had clearly been diverted away from the walking dead towards the penalties for trespass.

"Talking about zombies, here's Nixon. Watch it!"

Mr Nixon was our deputy head teacher. The truth was there was something a bit zombie-like about him. He was small, completely hairless, had dark rings under his eyes and the rumour was that there were dead kids in his stockroom. He was humourless too. And he barked. When he attempted what he thought was a smile you got the definite impression that he was preparing to bite you rather than be friendly.

He shouted or barked something from the other end of the corridor. He had this way of adding more letters to the end of every sentence. "Still chattering-ga in the corridor-ra when you should be thirsting-ga for knowledge in Mr Hetherington's class-sa. If I catch any of you, I'll have to bite a leg off by way of an example to the rest of the school-la!"

We turned to scatter.

"Not so fast. Halt!! I need a word – Victoria," he said, making this finger and thumb gesture as though he was picking her up by her ear or dangling her on a piece of string.

We all froze.

"I hear from Mrs Ditchfield that you and she had a conversation recently."

"Did we?" Victor looked puzzled.

"About chewing gum on the chairs in the hall?"

"Oh yes, sir. I got it all over my – the back - of my skirt."

"Yes, she said. You accused her of not doing her caretaking and cleaning job carefully enough."

"I didn't!" Victor was irate.

"She said you called her a punk!"

"I did not! I said that I was surprised that there was chewing gum on the chairs because she was usually so punctilious. I never said punk! I said punctilious – which means …."

"I know what it means, Victoria, thank you! Mrs Ditchfield, our hard working caretaker, is indeed punctilious, *if* that's what you said! Scrupulous. Meticulous. Mr Nixon, however, your all-seeing Deputy Head Teacher, is sceptical! Don't look so horrified, Arthur, just go into your classroom and look it up. Meanwhile, Victoria, I'm keeping my eye on you. You're far too quick to hit people over the head with big words. I think you've got a bit of a nasty streak in you. Hidden away, of course, behind those over-large eyes, which deceive people into thinking you are an innocent but I suspect conceal the fact that you've become a vocabulary thug!"

He strode off.

"Isn't that when you cut yourself and don't clean it properly and your cut goes all grungy and sceptical and it oozes out … Has Nixon got something that's gone sceptical? Will he have to go to hospital?"

"For goodness sake, Arthur! That's septic, not sceptical. Sceptical is when you don't believe people." Victor wasn't irate any more, she was exasperated. "I haven't got a nasty streak, have I?"

'No, course not, Victor, you're not nasty, ever," I said. 'A bit spiky sometimes, but not nasty."

"I'm not spiky!"

"If her words were cricket balls," Arthur said in a Mr Nixon voice, "she'd break-ka every bone-na in your body -a!"

"Arthur! That's not helpful."

Arthur was crestfallen, "I was only joking."

"You can be very quick with an answer, that's all we meant, Victor," offered Eric.

"I'll settle for quick. People like Nixon try to steal the bits of you they don't like, and replace them with bits that they do like. They don't like it when you use interesting words or ask difficult questions, so they tell you to stop it. In the end they're just trying to make you smaller!"

We said nothing. It was very easy to put your foot in it with Victor on the subject of what people expected of her, so you avoided it.

At which point, the classroom door burst open and Mr Hetherington popped his head out. "Did I hear Mr Nixon out here?"

"No, sir," I said. The others looked at me quizzically as if to say, "Why do you always deny everything, Jim, even when it's not important?"

Anyway, I don't know why Nixon was going on as though we were late, because when Mr Hetherington ushered us into his classroom, there was nobody there except Mr Hetherington who immediately went back to doing what he was always doing – drinking tea and eating something.

He was having a clean-shaven day, today. Some weeks he didn't shave at all and his beard grew and grew and then, without warning, he would turn up clean-shaven. I had this theory that he only had a shave when he went round to see his mother. He must have been really scared of her. She would say, "You haven't been growing one of them beards again, have you, our Kenny? Them as grow beards have something to hide, I always say."

And he would say, "No, Mum, honest." Then when he came back to school he would forget the promises he had made to his poor old mother and let the whiskers multiply all over his two faces – the one he had for his mother and the one he had for the rest of the world!

"Sir, sir," blurted out Arthur as though he had been bursting to ask this question for days and if he didn't say it now he might have a trouser accident, "Sir, how much was forty shillings worth when they had shillings?"

"Well – the answer is just over there, Arthur. It's called a computer and all you have to do is log on and ask your question."

"I thought you might be quicker."

"My job is to teach you *how* to learn, not to give you quick answers," Mr Hetherington said, rather smugly. I think he must have read that somewhere – or heard it on one of those courses he was always going on.

We all gathered around the computer and while Arthur was logging on, I whispered, "Do you think Nixon is a zombie? No hair, those teeth, the dead eyes. Did you hear what he said about biting people's legs off and did you notice this morning as he strode down the corridor towards us that there was a little, very tiny, slender trickle of blood coming from the corner of his mouth and down his chin?"

"What?" Arthur shot out of his seat and almost shouted. "Honestly? Say honestly!"

"That was quick," said Mr Hetherington. "What's the answer?"

When we all started laughing, Arthur plonked himself moodily back into his seat and got on with his search. "You're sick, you lot. Sick and wrong. I knew there was no blood!"

Mr Hetherington returned to his marking – well, I say marking, he was ticking somebody's work without even looking at it. Telepathic marking. Or sleepwalking marking.

Victor was thoughtful. "The thing about teachers is that they often aren't as old as we think they are."

"Nixon is," said Eric.

"He might not be. He might be no older than our parents,"

"How old are you, sir?" Eric called across to Mr Hetherington.

"Twenty one," Mr Hetherington said trying to sound genuine.

"No he isn't," whispered Victor. "If it wasn't for the erratic facial hair growth, I'd say he was about fifteen and that's on a day when he's really making an effort to be grown up. All I'm saying is you can't go on looks. Just because Nixon has got no hair..."

"And no sense of humour – or compassion," I added.

"It doesn't mean he's an old man."

"If he had children of his own," I said, "he might know how we felt. He might have some – what was that word, Victor, which means seeing things through other people's shoes?"

"Eyes, not shoes. You *walk* in other people's shoes. You *see* through other people's eyes. It's called *empathy* – when you can put yourself in some else's position. Like when Eric cries watching animated films about misunderstood animals."

"I do not!! Anyway, we weren't talking about how old Nixon is, we were talking about the 'Beware of the Trains' notice that Henley Phipps says he has." We moved across to Eric's desk and all sat down out of Mr Hetherington's hearing to listen to Eric, the railway expert. "It's a bit of a mystery, you know, all this from Henley. There's never been a railway at Crowton Mill from what I know. The nearest train line goes over Seven Arches Viaduct and the only station is on the other side of the river at West Norley – miles away. I know there were loads of tracks and stations closed in the 1960s by someone called Doctor Beeching but I've never heard of anything at Crowton Mill. But – but – on the other hand, Crowton Mill *is* about a mile and a half from where this estate's original village was and the big house, Crowton Manor, is only about half a mile on the other side of the Mill."

We all loved solving clues and this was looking promising. Victor said, "So you're saying that although we've never heard of a railway at Crowton Mill, it would be a perfect place to put a station? Close to the village but not in it, and even closer to the big house?"

"Exactly, but I still can't see the point. Where would the line come from and go to? What would it be for? I would have thought that Crowton Mill had stopped being an actual mill producing flour years before there were trains.

By the time steam trains were roaring through here, the mill had long gone I should think – and the village was too small for a station. There was no new housing estate tagged onto the original village until the 1980s."

"Twenty shillings to a pound, so forty shillings would be two pounds," called Arthur triumphantly.

"Yes, but what was it worth? That's the point! What could you do with two pounds when it was made up of forty shillings? " said Eric in an 'answer that' kind of voice.

"You could pay your fine for walking on the railway, of course!" answered Arthur in his 'checkmate' kind of voice.

"You could ask Mr Nixon," said Mr Hetherington. We'd forgotten he was still in the room, "about the railway. He's always lived around here, and his parents and his grandparents. He'd know if there was ever a railway at Crowton Mill – or he could find out."

With that, Mr Hetherington went out to round up the rest of our class from the playground.

"What do you think?" I said.

"No. We couldn't," said Eric. "Not Nixon. It wouldn't be right even trying to have a normal conversation with him. He'd be sceptical, think we were trying to have him on. But – but – we could just go and have a look around. We don't have to go with Henley Phipps or anybody else. Just the four of us. It would be like an archaeological expedition. Like looking for Tutankhamen in a lost railway station."

Victor snorted. "I think you're stretching it a bit there, Eric. I don't think we'll find Tutankhamen waiting for a train in the woods behind Crowton Mill."

"You never know. Anything is possible - even the corpse of an Egyptian king sitting in a waiting room. Even zombies?"

"I don't think that's funny, Eric," said Arthur as he got out his books for first lesson. "Not funny at all."

****

7.

Crowton Mill

You know how some weeks are just ordinary and how other weeks are *extra*ordinary and how very occasionally some weeks are *beyond* extraordinary? Well this week, the one where the decision was made to excavate Crowton Mill, was ordinary - hollow and colourless ordinary like being sent to bed for days with no books and the curtains closed; with the sun shining outside and the sounds of kids playing in the distance and you banished from real life.

We didn't even talk about going to Crowton Mill on the next Saturday because talking about it seemed to make time go backwards and the weariness of the days feel even heavier. We knew, or at least suspected, that once we got onto our bikes and rode the mile and a half to Crowton Mill, the ordinariness of the week would be wiped away, like when screen wash is squirted and windscreen wipers wipe. The murk would disappear and we would start seeing things again and they would be *interesting* things.

Coming off the tarmacked road onto the sporadically muddy track that led up to the mill from the main road made all of us go quiet. You could see, here and there, small groups of cobblestones underneath the weeds and water of the track. Actually, we didn't really know if we were allowed to go down this lane, whether it may be private: no public right of way; trespassers will be shouted at – or shot – or fined whatever forty shillings was worth in this year's money.

So we just wheeled our bikes down the lane in silence.

You could feel the water of the mill pond before you could see it. It was something about the light catching the trees and the slight dip in temperature. Then we did see it. The trees and the sky perfectly reflected in the absolutely motionless water. I know it's a cliché to say that one was a mirror image of the other, but actually, one *was* a perfect mirror image of the other. If you stood on your head to look at it, you still wouldn't know which was real and which reflection. Which was up and which was down.

Already, the 'ordinary' wasn't there anymore. We'd left it behind at the road end of the muddy track.

The very tall mill building was to our left and the mill pond to our right. On the side of the building boxed in with dark wood, you could see where the mill wheel had been, or still was for all we knew, but there was no sound of it turning. On the far side of the pond, the track veered sharply left in front of a steep and over-grown embankment.

I couldn't resist it. Perhaps I was excited, perhaps – more likely – I just felt released, but I wanted to be the first to race up the embankment and discover that long forgotten railway track running along the top. So I did. I ran, I hurtled, full speed ahead! I didn't even look to see how the others were reacting, I just threw myself down the last few yards of the lane and up the slope – which was, of course, twice as steep and twice as matted with vegetation as I had imagined. Nevertheless, I was committed. Driven. Fearless. Heroic. I was certain the others would follow once they saw my determination and caught my excitement. If I had a sword I would be pointing it straight ahead of me and roaring, "Charge!" then waving it round in circles over my head shouting, "Follow me, lads!" Of course, I didn't do either. I didn't have the sword – and I didn't have the breath for shouting anything.

My run became a walk; or rather a sort of crawl so steep was the embankment. I didn't want to stop and I didn't want to look back. Then, part way I looked up hoping I was almost at the top.

The sun was in my eyes as it fragmented its way through the trees which lined the top of the bank and I was certain that there was a *person* there, a sort of silhouette distorted by the sun's rays from behind, but definitely a person! Perhaps the others had found another way up except whoever it was up there was wearing a cap. My lot didn't wear caps. I looked back, no sign of them. I looked up – no silhouette. Despite the washing machine in my stomach sensation, again, I pressed on, trying not to make that noise you make on the toilet when – you know – when you are trying to achieve what you came in there for and for some reason it's hard work.

At the top of the slope not only were there no railway lines, but also no person or people. My chest hurt. My lungs were trying to get out, I think. Then the thought came – I've been here before. Not here – at Crowton Mill: in this situation, a couple of nights ago in our garden playing kick-the-can when I was hiding and they all cleared off and left me. It had happened again. I'd been left on my own – with someone watching me – out there inside those shadows. Only this time there would be no kitchen light coming on.

I had to go home. This wasn't a magical secret place at all! It was creepy. Too still. Too shadowy. Too – and I was falling, sliding, rolling back down the embankment towards the lane. I would get my bike and go as fast as I could pedal, never mind the mud and the puddles, never mind the others. They would have to manage without me.

Before I could prepare myself, I was bursting out of the undergrowth, so fast that one of my legs buckled under me and I fell. As got to my feet, saying, "Ow, ow, ow" over and over, I looked up and saw Victor, Arthur and Eric standing in a line facing me.

In front of them there was a boy: not just white hair but white eyebrows and flour-white skin, and a round face and – the strangest thing of all – eyes. Henley was wrong; he definitely had eyes, but not just eyes like anybody else's eyes, like my eyes or Victor's massive eyes. His eyes had no colour in them at all!

This kid had transparent eyes.

****

8.

The Boy with Transparent Eyes

It was like looking at a photograph. Eric, Arthur, Victor and this boy with transparent eyes all motionless and looking at me, as though they were posing waiting for someone to take a picture.

Then Arthur broke the silence. "Did you just fall out of the sky? You frightened us to death!"

"And you were talking to yourself," said Eric, "Again! Where've you been?"

"I wasn't talking to myself. I've just fallen all the way down that massive hill."

"Embankment," said the kid, coming across to stand by me. "That's called the embankment. You go up to the top, walk down a path and you get to the house. Crowton Manor. If that's where you were trying to go."

I found myself looking at his mouth. I didn't think zombies could talk – apart from making like 'uuhhhh' noises and walking towards you making grabbing gestures with their arms. This kid was talking. In English, so he probably wasn't even an alien. He looked like an alien – all that whiteness and everything – but otherwise I think he was quite similar to us, same height roughly, same age roughly, same mouth and ears – limbs – he had the lot. It was just all the whiteness. His clothes weren't white. He was. Maybe he was a ghost? Or - perhaps the mill still did do flour and he'd fallen in it? There were no white footprints though. I don't think he was a ghost either. Behind or inside the whiteness I think he was a real person – apart from the transparent eyes.

I don't know how long these thoughts took but I suddenly realised that they were all looking at me, waiting for me to speak.

"Was it you up at the top of the – embankment – in the trees?" I said, remembering the silhouette that had caused my panic and plummet through the air – well, through the vegetation anyway, "I thought I sounded more hostile than I meant to so I added, "I thought I saw – there was …."

"No. I've been here talking to Eric and Arthur and Victor."

He knew their names already!

Victor helped me out as she always did. She could sense that my mind was racing and roaring with questions, so she stepped in with some clarification. "Jim, this is Rembrandt."

"Rembrandt, Jim, Rembrandt!" exploded Arthur pointing from one of us to the other. "How about that for a fantastic name, Jim! The most lost of all the lost names."

"Is that after the painter?" I asked

"What painter?"

"Dutch painter, I think."

"No, I don't think so."

"Which school do you go to?" I asked trying to sound normal.

"He doesn't even go to school, Jimmy." said Arthur sounding even more impressed. "It's because of your name, I bet. Isn't it?" he added turning to Rembrandt and trying to sound understanding. "We have that, don't we, men?"

"My name's Jim," I said to Rembrandt. "No one calls me Jimmy."

"And lives!" laughed Arthur.

"So is that allowed? Not going to school? Just because of your name?"

"That's not why I don't go to school. It's because of the way I look."

"What do you mean, the way you look?" I said slightly overdoing the disbelief, "You look all right to us, doesn't he?" They all looked at me with a fairly obvious scepticism, with looks that said, "What are you talking about?" so I repeated, "He looks normal, doesn't he?" I was nodding vigorously just to make sure they got it.

"Oh yeah, normal."

"Definitely normal."

"Nothing like a zombie."

"Arthur!!" we all said more or less simultaneously.

"I meant blondie, didn't I? Blondie. Did I say something else? You're very fair though, aren't you?"

You know that saying about when you're in a hole, stop digging? Arthur had never heard that saying, obviously, just like me mixing up walking in other people's shoes or seeing through other people's eyes. We all knew he would just keep talking and it would become more and more embarrassing for the kid and for all of us.

"Because," Eric interrupted, desperately trying to think of something to say that would change the subject, "We heard there used to be a train station here. So we thought we could come and do some archaeology, like, find out if it's true."

The kid made one of those 'don't know' faces and hunched his shoulders. That was the end of that line of conversation then.

So Victor brought us back to what we all really wanted to ask. "You don't go to school at all?"

"I'm educated at home, everything – reading, numeracy, writing, history - in our house."

Victor was impressed. "All your lessons. Even PE?"

"We don't do all that much PE, no."

"Is that allowed?" enthused Arthur, who has a very short memory and obviously felt it was now safe to talk again.

"What? Not doing much PE?"

"No. Having all your lessons in your own private house. What do you do for a teacher? Don't you have teachers? That would be so cool, wouldn't it, not having teachers. They can be very unpredictable, teachers. We have one who keeps changing his mind about whether or not he should grow a beard and he goes on all the time about tests and, when we get really interested in something he says, "You won't write about that on your test paper, will you?" and he goes all panicky – which makes him eat twice as much at playtime. And - I don't think he even understands about healthy eating ...."

Victor raised her arm. "You can stop now, Arthur. How many times have I got to tell you that when you ask someone a question, you're supposed to give them space to answer it? So, Rembrandt," she went on sounding like a BBC interviewer, "How does it work? Educated at home?"

"My mother teaches me, sets the work, anyway. We do lessons all morning then in the afternoon I can choose what to do, or go with my mum to where she works, and then when my dad comes home, he marks what I've done."

"And that's allowed?" said Eric.

"I asked that," protested Arthur.

"My parents had to apply to teach me at home and have an interview. Then someone comes round every now and again to check that I'm up to where I should be for my age with reading, writing and numeracy."

"Nothing else?"

"Not really. I show them my other work, but they're not really interested. Just what's on the tests."

"Typical," said Arthur with feeling.

By this time the conversation was becoming less like an interview and more like a relaxed chat. We were walking now, across the large paved area which fronted the tall mill building and towards the muddy track we had come down earlier.

"My mum works at the house. Crowton Manor. She's like a sort of housekeeper or caretaker so can come and go to suit herself. No one lives there now. It's still all furnished and kept nice, sort of, but the family who used to live there live all over the place. Down south, abroad. This is their sort of holiday place now, but they hardly ever come. They used to own some farms and a big bakery in the town but I think it's all sold off now. Just the house."

"Bit bigger than a caravan or a cottage, isn't it?" said Eric.

"Mmmm."

Then Victor asked the big question. The unspoken question. The question we all wanted to ask but didn't quite know how. "So," she said, "why *exactly* don't you go to school?"

"I tried for quite a long time, but it was too hard. The other kids. Look at me." We all looked. "What do I look like?"

"A kid," said Victor.

"You are a bit sort of white everywhere," Arthur again.

"Arthur!"

"But he is!"

"No, he's right. I am very white, exceptionally white. It's called Albinism. I'm albino."

"Is that a country?" said Arthur.

"It's when you have some pigments missing - you know, from the chemicals that you're made up of, so you look like this. When I went to school, they stared at me all the time, or some of the little kids cried when they saw me and some of the big kids kept threatening to beat me up. Some of them said I was an alien or a zombie so they would have to defend planet earth against me. Once I heard my mum and dad talking and saying that some parents had contacted the school to say they thought it wasn't right for me to be with their kids. I ought to be in a special school."

"Which you are, really. Here. Being educated at home. That's pretty special," I said.

"It's the only other choice. There's no reason why there should be a special school for me just because I look a bit…"

"Unique?" For once Arthur said something that we could all agree with and smile at.

"Anyway, I don't mind. At least I don't lie in bed at night worrying about what might happen or be said the next day. It's quieter at home – and I think my parents probably make me do more work than I'd have to do at school. No-one to hide behind here, no-one else in the room to divert the attention away from me."

There was a pause. I suppose we were all thinking the same thing. Would we like to have a life like this kid's life? It had its attractions, but…always on your own, always quiet?

"Time we went," said sensible Victor.

Eric groaned, "But we didn't even look for the long lost train station."

"Come tomorrow and I'll show you," said Rembrandt.

You know at the end of an episode of something on the telly when everyone's mouth drops open and then the picture freezes and you go, 'Oh no, how can I possibly wait for the next episode?"

That's what happened when Rembrandt said that about showing us the long lost train station tomorrow. Only this wasn't on the television, it wasn't episodes and it definitely was not a made up story. It was real.

****

9.

Once seen

It might have been the fall down the embankment but as we trudged up the muddy lane leading from Crowton Mill, I developed this ringing in my head. Like a telephone. It might have been a warning, it might have been my conscience, it might have been someone trying to communicate some vital information to me, it might have been emotional overload or it might just have been a headache.

I had seen the albino kid. We had spoken to each other. He had been bullied just like me, only worse probably. He knew the location of the lost railway and one of its stations. He was educated at home! And he definitely wasn't a zombie.

What I had seen could not be unseen. What I had heard could not be unheard. I am not sure which information was worse: all this from the boy with transparent eyes called Rembrandt or the shadow I thought I saw at the top of the embankment, or that bottomless feeling I had when I was trapped in the hedge the other night or what I had seen and heard when we visited Henley Phipps in his blacked-out bedroom. The scars. The agony drawings. The darkness in his room. The darkness in his head! Then, it had always been dark in Henley Phipps' head. No lights in there at all, ever.

With normal people, frightening dreams come into their heads when they're asleep; mine seemed to be coming into my head when I was awake!

I wondered what Henley Phipps would do if he found out that we'd come to Crowton Mill without him? Roar probably and flail about uncontrollably. He might even report us to the five-a-day estate head-case, Chucky Locket and ask him to 'sort us out'! There was no way we could bring Henley Phipps here, though. How would he cope with Rembrandt? He would never understand that Rembrandt wasn't a zombie, or an alien, or a threat to the human race. He would never accept that Rembrandt was actually from round here and was just like us, except he didn't go to school.

"He didn't sound as though he was having us on, did he though?" said Victor who had obviously been thinking about the lost railway.

"Anyone with a name like Rembrandt wouldn't tell lies," Eric insisted. "People with a lost name do not make things up. Well, they do make things up, but they don't tell lies."

Arthur was a few feet ahead of us; head down over his handlebars. As he pushed his bike up the lane he began to shout:

"This is the night train crossing the border
Bringing the cheque and the postal order,
Letters for the rich, letters for the poor,
The shop at the corner and the girl next door."

It was a poem he had been trying to learn, called 'Night Mail' by Wystan Hugh Auden. Another cool lost name, Wystan.

"I'm very impressed by your amazing memory and very loud voice, Arthur, but what's a postal order?" said Eric.

"Don't you remember those stories we found in the church bring and buy sale about Billy Bunter, that big kid with the little round glasses – a bit like Chucky Lockett only with a posh school uniform. They were in a pile of old and cardboardy books with things written inside the front cover like, 'To George, on your 10th birthday: July 1948, from your Aunty Betty.' You must remember."

"Yes – but what's a postal order?"

Victor explained: "It comes in the post and you buy 'tuck' with it if you're Billy Bunter."

"What's tuck?" said Eric.

And we all shouted, "Eric! Shut up!" simultaneously.

This gave Arthur permission to go on:

"The chatty, the catty, the boring, adoring,
The cold and official and the heart's outpouring,
Clever, stupid, short and long,
The typed and the printed and the spelt all wrong."

"Those spelt all wrong letters'll be from Henley Phipps," I said and immediately felt mean for saying it.

"That was unnecessary," said Victor, as if I didn't know.

We reached the road. Arthur mounted his bike and pushed down on his pedals, shouting as he went:

"Past cotton grass and moorland boulder
Shovelling white steam over her shoulder."

Nothing else was said about what was on all of our minds: tomorrow and what would happen when we went back to Crowton Mill. *If* we went back to Crowton Mill. We rode home, still in the same single line as we had been in as we'd trudged up the Crowton Mill lane pushing our bikes. Only this time much, much faster.

Eric peeled off first to go into his house, and then Arthur, then Victor and each one shouting as they braked and mounted the pavement in front of their houses: "See you in the morning. About ten."

Once said, it couldn't be unsaid. Once arranged, it couldn't be unarranged.

Crowton Mill, the next day. Someone turned on the washing machine in my stomach again. Once felt, it couldn't be unfelt!

****

10.

Fretwork Valences

Standing there at Crowton Mill, looking at it all, I was disturbed not so much by what *was* there as by what *wasn't* there. By what ought to be there! I don't just mean the people who would have once worked there, or those who might still be there like the silhouette I saw the day before as I climbed the embankment, or Rembrandt, I mean the buildings and the roads, all the bricks and metal and wires that would have been there if it had in fact been a train station. I couldn't see those cream coloured roofs with the patterned canopies over the platforms, or the signal boxes, or the waiting room or the ticket office, or the fire buckets, but I just knew they were there – or at least that they were once there and I could definitely still feel the space in the air that they had left when they disappeared – feel it as though time hadn't passed, it had just caused things to go – sort of – out of focus.

"They were called fretwork valences," a voice behind me said. It was Rembrandt, not looking at me but across the mill pond towards the embankment on the far side.

Had I been talking to myself? Had he heard me rambling on about what I imagined was once there?

"What were?" I said.

"Those roofs over the platform had a sort of frilly edging which was called a fretwork valence. And there would have been a goods shed with a tariff board at the end of a siding round the back, and on the platform there was like a wooden shelf where they left milk churns, and one platform would have been the Up platform to West Norley and all points north, and the other platform, the Down platform, to Turner's Bridge and the south. And on both platforms, there would have been big cast iron signs with raised letters that said Crowton Halt – and a few seats – and a few potted plants and hanging baskets - and probably a cat."

"Did you see all that, or did someone tell you?"

"I didn't see it, no. I just felt it, like you; imagined it, anyway - guessed."

"Who told you I felt it?"

"What did you see at the top of the embankment, yesterday?"

"Nothing!" Sometimes my instinct to lie or deny when asked a question would so embarrass me, I would go red.

"Didn't you see, like a long flat road with sleeper indentations in the grass?"

"Railway lines?"

"Yeah – you can see them if you look. It was called the track, not lines. It was lifted a long time ago. There're just these indentations where the sleepers would have been. Didn't you see them? Or were you too spooked by the man?"

"What man?"

"Didn't your mother tell you it was rude to answer a question with a question? I don't know if you saw a man or not. I was just guessing again. Was he wearing a cap? Some of them wear caps."

"Them? Are there blokes working round here – in the mill or somewhere?"

"The mill is closed. The big house is mostly closed, except when my mum goes in there to clean and check things like pigeons falling down the chimney or gutters leaking. I don't think there are supposed to be blokes here at all."

There was no answer to that, so I said, "Umm! Anyway – wait till I tell the others about the sleeper thingies."

"Indentations."

"Right." There was a pause. "So who is the bloke with the cap? I did see him. I don't know why I didn't admit it – I just do things like that. Did *you* think it was your imagination?"

Rembrandt looked pleased for a second, and then tried to hide his delight at having found someone he could talk to about what he'd seen. So he was off, the words spilling out at a hundred miles an hour. "I knew it wasn't just me. I'm sure there's more than one bloke actually. Perhaps it's travellers from somewhere in the woods or poachers, I don't know. The men I've seen – you've seen – wear a cap and a tie – and their jackets and trousers are dark coloured - black maybe."

"What do they say to you?"

He looked appalled. "I've never spoken to them. I'm never that close to them and anyway – what did the man you saw look like?"

"The sun was in my eyes and I was out of breath…."

"Exactly! It's always the same. You never quite see them. They're always just that bit too far away, or the light is going, or you've just caught the back of them going behind something."

"I bet it's poachers," I said trying to convince myself as much as Rembrandt. "I bet you've loads of things here they could catch, and there are hardly any people to disturb them. They wouldn't want to be seen would they, you know, run off when they see someone?"

"No."

I'd almost turned into Victor, all common sense and logic. "Or train spotters – wondering what time the next train will come."

Rembrandt laughed. "They'll have a long wait."

"Talking of which, that looks like Eric and Arthur and Victor. Oi, you lot! We're here. Oi!"

"Don't shout! My mum and dad'll hear you. It is Sunday, you know."

"Sorry!" I made do with waving my arms about to attract their attention.

Eric, Arthur and Victor were pushing their bikes down the last part of the muddy lane and out onto the paved area in front of the mill. Arthur was bringing up the rear and was trying to brush their tracks away with a branch from a tree. Why were they all together? That was not what we'd said we'd do! We had arranged to bike it to Crowton Mill separately just in case Henley Phipps, or worse, Chucky Lockett, were on a mission to track us down – or even just be here by coincidence - come by themselves for a bit of illicit fishing. A bit of sly poaching! Come to that, perhaps the elusive people shapes were in fact Henley Phipps and Chucky Lockett, both wearing caps pulled down over their faces to hide their identities – and their scars!

"Were you in my back garden that time," I asked, "when the others had gone and it was nearly dark?"

"I might have been."

"And just now, were you really reading my mind about the what-do-you-call-it fretwork canopy things?"

"Valences. I might have been."

Considering this kid had transparent eyes you'd think you might be able to see into his head and discover what he was thinking – but you couldn't. All you saw in his eyes was your own reflection - looking out.

"A coincidence," said Victor when she got close enough. "We bumped into each other on the main road just near the pub. No one was following us, don't worry."

"We didn't actually bump into each other, we sort of merged," Eric said bringing his hands together in a merging gesture.

"And – did you notice - I rubbed out our bike tracks down the lane," said Arthur proudly, "with this branch. Like a Native American tracker. We are now invisible. Untraceable!"

"Arthur, Eric, I've got something to tell you," I said trying to cover up my unease about Rembrandt. "There are indentations!"

"You what!" said Arthur.

"Indentations. In the grass where the sleepers were – which proves ..."

"There was a railway line!" Eric exploded and he paced around in circles wondering which way to run. "Where? Where? Let's go, come on! Quick! Come on! Tutankhamen? Orrrr, man! This is mega!"

"Track not lines," I said trying to sound cool but failing because of the row they were making.

Eric and Arthur were jumping up and down and looking as though they were about to grab each other and start dancing. Even Victor looked excited – for her. She was smiling and showing her teeth. She never did that. There was nothing wrong with her teeth; she just didn't let them be seen very often.

Only Rembrandt was still. He was waiting for the excitement to subside. "The thing is," he said, "if you really want to see everything, you're going to have to take a few risks. Be a bit brave."

"I'm brave," said Arthur. "Ask anybody."

"Okay, follow me." Rembrandt headed off between the mill and the water and towards the steep embankment. We followed.

I didn't like the sound of that word 'brave'. It usually meant reckless or mad or stupid – and it probably was going to involve something that would make me look like the scared-of-my-own shadow sort of person I knew I was – but tried to hide from everyone else. I hoped this wasn't about poachers again, with caps.

It looked as though we were in for a climb, but when we reached the foot of the embankment Rembrandt turned to the right and with the mill behind us we walked along the bottom edge of the hill. He stopped and gestured towards a low growing bush which was only a few feet up the slope. "In there," he said.

"In where?" I said.

Rembrandt took hold of the bush and lifted it, right away from the grass, like a magician or a chef revealing a spectacular trick or plate of food. The bush, roots soil and all, had been concealing a small circular hole – like a tunnel only very, very small. "The train station is down there," he said seriously.

"You couldn't get a train station down that hole! Or a train! Or even a person probably. Not even Arthur," said Victor.

"What you've come for is down there. Are you ready?"

I don't even know why I am telling this story. The very thought of it rekindles the horror. Standing there, feeling more than anything like running for it, I wanted to tell the nightmare pictures in my head to clear off – to come back when I was asleep, not now. At least when you're asleep you can wake up. This time it wasn't like a washing machine in my stomach, it was more like a block of ice; a feeling like that feeling I got looking at Henley Phipps' profile through the miniscule gap in his bedroom door and being certain that I was looking at a dead body. It not only felt like looking into a darkness that was bottomless, the actual hole looked bottomless and all I could hear was Rembrandt's calm voice asking if we were ready. I didn't even look at the others. I couldn't take my eyes off that dark tunnel.

Arthur said, "In there? Honestly? Say honestly!"

"It looks like a rabbit burrow to me," said Eric, "not a people burrow."

I was aware of Victor looking at me. I don't know if she was waiting for me to make a decision about whether or not we all ought to slither into this impossibly small tunnel or whether she was sensing my horror at the thought of going in there at all. I'd never actually said anything about how scared I was of small dark spaces, but I think Victor knew. She definitely knew I used to have nightmares about the ceiling in my bedroom falling down in the night and smothering me, so she probably worked out that I was really quite badly claustrophobic. She had a very good empathy gland did Victor and she never turned it off.

"Howard Carter must have had the same hesitations," said Rembrandt, "when he was standing outside the tunnel that would lead him to Tutankhamen's tomb."

"You sound like the voice-over in a documentary," said Victor and, picking up on the David Attenborough voice, went on: "Little did the intrepid explorer know what riches and wonders awaited him at the end of that dark and dangerous tunnel."

"And that was a tomb," Rembrandt said encouragingly. "A grave covered by a pyramid, with bodies. There are no bodies in there."

"Yet!" I said, surprised that my voice actually worked.

"I'll do it," said Arthur.

"Arthur!" Victor was appalled. "You know nothing about it. What is it, Rembrandt? How far in does it go? What's at the other end – and – and – once you're squashed in there, how do you turn around to get out?"

That thought about not being able to turn around to get out made it very hard for me to breathe. I was gasping for breath, mouth open, eyes closed.

"If Arthur goes in, I'll go in," said Eric. "I don't mind."

Victor was more agitated than I'd ever seen her. "Rembrandt! If these two kids get buried in an embankment when they're not even dead, you'll be in big trouble! I'll tell everyone you made them do it. Talk about educated at home; you'll be educated in a flipping prison."

Rembrandt didn't flinch. "I'll come too, you know. I've been in before. The tunnel isn't all that long and there *is* a space to turn around when you get to the end."

"So you say!"

"Would I come with you, if I thought we couldn't get out?"

"That's the sort of trick Henley Phipps would play."

"And Chucky Lockett."

"All right then, I'll go first," said Rembrandt and he crouched down to enter the tunnel.

"No! Me first! I want to be the first. 'I was the first that ever burst into that silent sea'," said Arthur. It was another one of those poems he had a habit of learning and with that he fell to his knees and began to crawl into the tunnel. The tunnel was so narrow it clearly wasn't easy to move forward. You were flat on your stomach so couldn't crawl, which meant Arthur had to sort of wriggle, arms stretched out in front of him, fingers waving about in the darkness, toes behind pushing into the soil and moving him forward an inch at a time.

Then, unexpectedly, Rembrandt grabbed Arthur's ankles and pulled him back out.

"What?" said Arthur, already unused to the light after the darkness he'd just left.

"I forgot," said Rembrandt. "Two things. First, the rule is that if *one* goes down there we *all* go..."

Victor gave me a sharp look jolting me into finding just about enough breath to say, "So there are no witnesses?"

"And second – you'll need this." He handed Arthur a small, slim torch. "So that you can see in the dark. When you get to the end, turn around and shine the torch back into the tunnel so that whoever comes next can see."

Arthur grinned. His face was filthy already. Once again he fell to his knees and carefully wriggled into the dark.

It was like when you see paratroopers waiting to jump from the aeroplane and there's a sergeant or someone tapping each one on the shoulder to tell him it's his turn and he hurls himself out into the sky and is swept away instantly by the force of the wind and the speed of the aircraft. Eric stood there by the tunnel waiting to be tapped on the shoulder by Rembrandt. The tap came. He sank to his knees, shouted into the hole, "Arthur, I'm coming," and wriggled into the darkness.

I was horrified. "What if Arthur's stuck down there and Eric comes up behind him and then he won't be able to go any further – or come back! They'll both suffocate"

"That won't happen," said Rembrandt. "Who's next? Jimmy? Victor? Or do you want me to go next?"

"It's your tunnel, and anyway, it's Jim, not Jimmy," I said.

"Right! And it's Rem. Not Rembrandt or Remmy. Rem."

And he was gone. I looked at Victor.

"If you're thinking of making a run for it, Jim, forget it. You can't let a bit of dark split up the lost names gang. It can't be as bad as being sent to Nixon's office and having to wait for hours in the corridor, or facing up to Henley Phipps when he's after you, or when we went to see him in his bedroom and thought he was dead and had to look at all those scars and see his drawings and listen to all those words he had to describe the pain. A bit of dark is nothing compared to all that. And anyway, if Arthur and Eric get trapped down there and disappear, we'll have to tell their mums and they're bound to blame us – and they'd probably cry – and they'd make a complaint to the school and we'd get sent to Nixon's office again…"

"All right! All right! But I'm not going first. You go first. And once you're in I'll follow. But, please, please, please whatever you do keep going, don't stop. If you stop I'll think we're stuck and I'll panic and start thinking about all the soil up over my head and how it's all going to collapse..."

"Goodness sake, Jim! Pack it in. Just turn your brain off for a few minutes."

Victor gave me the thumbs up sign and went. I followed her straight away thinking, "Don't think about it, don't think about it, just do it, keep moving, keep moving, don't forget to breathe, go faster Victor, go faster.... breath breathe..."

The only way to move was to wriggle and push with your toes. It was so tight and each movement only produced about a centimetre of progress, but as long as I only thought about the movement and nothing else it was okay.

Then, my head hit Victor's feet. She had stopped. Nothing. No light. No sound.

The thoughts started. All that soil above me waiting to just thunder down on my head – just like my bedroom ceiling did over and over when I was asleep. I've got to get out. Why did you stop, Victor? You've let the thoughts in. I've got to get out! But however hard I tried I couldn't do a backwards wriggle, my toes could not make a reverse movement happen. Despite my thrashing about toes and wriggling body and the screaming inside my head, my face remained firmly pressed against the soles of Victor's shoes.

So I stopped. I tried to stay still and breathe and listen to my heart beating - so hard it hurt my head.

What if the air ran out? I'd read stories where the air ran out! Stop it! Goodness sake, James McConkey, just stop it! What is the matter with your brain? Why does it always click into panic mode at the slightest thing? What do you mean the slightest thing? This wasn't a slight thing! This was a massive thing. I was stuck down a hole, unable to move, with the roof of a tunnel about to cave in on me and the air about to run out! And – Victor in front of me – she might even be dead – was – was - beginning to move – she was actually moving and I could see little splinters of light from the torch sneaking through on either side of Victor's wriggling body.

We were out. All of us. I knew the embankment was too massive for us to have burrowed right through it to the other side, so expected we'd end up in a sort of cave in the earth where we could turn around and get back – and I still needed to get out as soon as possible - now, please, I need to get out now! Having a bit more space doesn't help, not at all!!

Rembrandt took the torch from Arthur and shone it around the space. It wasn't an earthen cave, it had proper walls and a ceiling, and it was all covered in those old blue and white tiles with a sort of tulip pattern on them. "This was the subway under the station," he said, his voice producing a slight echo as he spoke. "Crowton Manor was a big rich house and when people came to visit they came to this station. The railway company built a special branch line leading off from the main line. The branch was called the Crowton Loop, and the station, Crowton Halt, and when the people needed to be on one or other platform they got to it by going underneath, through this subway. And when the mill was going full pelt they had a bit of extra track called the Crowton sidings where they had goods trains. This was a major place, in a way. A rich place anyway. Quite a few people worked here. The station had a complete team of workers."

Arthur and Eric were transfixed, so much so that Arthur tried to join in with Rembrandt's knowledge. "And then in the 1960s Dr Beeching came and closed it all down! The Beeching cuts. All the branch lines – all the loops - gone."

"It closed a long time before then," said Rembrandt. "I'll show you."

He led us further along the subway. There were bits of crunchy rumble on the floor, but the walls were as good as new; there were even some of those travel posters on the wall encouraging people to travel with the London Midland and Scottish Railway to the Peak District, Southport or North Wales.

"See that one there?" said Rembrandt reading a big red poster, "'For the thrill of your life and the holiday too: TT Races, Isle of Man'. That's why I'm called Rembrandt. After Harry Rembrandt Fowler the motorbike racer, won the first Isle of Man Tourist Trophy in 1907. My great, great grandfather was a big fan so called his son Rembrandt, and his grandson got called Rembrandt – and his great grandson – right down to my dad and me. All Rembrandt or Rem for short."

No one even said, 'Cool' although we all thought it. We were transfixed by this story, and then even more transfixed by what happened next.

Rembrandt took us to a flight of stairs, blue and white tiles up both sides and a dark wooden banister running up the middle. On the wall near the lowest step was a list of names, written in ink or it might even have been paint.

Rembrandt shone his torch on them and read:

October 1914
Stanley Greenhouse, booking clerk
Freddie Ditchfield, porter
Charlie Thurlwell, lengthman.
Phineas George Hewitt, guard.
Alfred Davenport, signalman.
Ted Buckley, footplate.
Len Hodgkinson, driver.
Percy Rembrandt Nixon, station foreman.
Envelope, the horse

There was a pause, and then Arthur said, "Was that allowed in those days, writing on walls?"

"Look at the date," said Victor. "Isn't that just a few weeks after the start of the First World War?"

"They all wrote their names on the wall before they left the station to sign up. They didn't have to. Working on the railway was called a 'reserved occupation' which meant they were needed to stay here and keep the railway going. But they wanted to fight for their country – or maybe they just wanted a bit of excitement away from here?"

"Did any of them come back after the war?"

"A couple did I think, most didn't. Same as up at the house. Most of the male servants and the gardeners didn't come back. That's when the house got closed up - and the station. There was no point in it being here when the people were gone. That was about 1919 or 1920."

"Hang on," said Eric. "There's a Rembrandt here on this list."

"My great, great grandfather. He was the Harry Rembrandt Fowler fan– which explains why he signed himself Percy Rembrandt. He even had a Norton motorbike. Everyone after him was actually christened Rembrandt."

"But his name's Percy Rembrandt *Nixon*."

"Same as mine," said Rembrandt. "He was in charge of the station before the war. Never came back from France. He left a wife and a baby son."

In the torch light, we could just about see each other's faces. Nixon? Nixon? The name bounced off the blue tiles of the walls and around our heads. "Can't be," said Eric out loud. "It just can't be the same family!"

****

11.

Crowton Manor

After the name Nixon had stopped echoing in our brains, we spent the next few minutes standing in that circle of torchlight around the list of names; every one of us thinking, probably, that those really were lost names up there on the wall. Then it dawned on us gradually that quite of few of these *names* weren't actually lost, even if the owners of them were. It wasn't just the name Nixon that was familiar; most of the names were names we recognised from the five-a-day estate and the old village. Mrs Ditchfield was the caretaker at our school; Jennifer Greenhouse lived about three doors from me; the newspaper shop was called Hodgkinson's and there were kids called Thurlwell and Hewitt in our class.

I'd even stopped thinking about how I was going to face that tunnel again when a voice broke the silence. "Remmy? Remmy? Are you down there?" It was a woman's voice and it was not coming from the tunnel but from somewhere up above.

"Is there another way to get in here?" I said in disbelief. "There is, isn't there? And you made us crawl down that nightmare tunnel!"

"You just go up these steps and you're out in the open," said Rem and even in that feeble light I could see his white hair and big toothy grin.

Unbelievable! I wonder if he had any idea what I'd gone through – but all I said was, "Who's that woman? Is it your mother?"

"Remmy! I know you're down there. How many times have I told you to answer when you're called?"

Rembrandt led the way up the stairs, round the corner and sure enough, tiny bars of day light were pushing their way through a tangle of bushes and trees. On the other side there stood a woman looking a bit annoyed.

"She looks a bit annoyed," whispered Victor to Rembrandt as we struggled through the undergrowth.

"Hi, Mum. These are my new friends: Jim, Eric, Arthur and Victor."

"She's a girl though, isn't she?" his mother said a bit suspiciously.

Victor smiled, showing her teeth yet again, blushed and looked really embarrassed. "My proper name is Victoria." I don't think I'd ever heard her admit that before!

Remmy's mum relaxed and smiled too. "I see. Remmy's proper name is Rembrandt."

"Actually, Remmy's proper name is Rem!" said Rem.

"Yes, he told us his name," I said, making every effort to speak very clearly and politely. "We came here looking for the old railway station. I don't think anyone round here knows about it at all. It's brilliant. I hope you don't mind."

"No, it's okay. Remmy doesn't see many children of his own age. Do you want to stay for a bit? I was just calling him in for a snack – I've got enough if you want to come up to the house and have a look round. If you've been down to the subway you've probably seen all that's left of the station, but you could have a look at the house."

"Fantastic," said Arthur.

"Brilliant," said Eric.

The subway steps had brought us out at the top of the embankment. We crossed where the track had been and saw the indentations, and even saw, here and there, small remnants of brickwork where the station buildings had stood, the occasional cracked paving slab and eroded tarmac.

Rembrandt and his family lived in a small part of the big house, round the side. There was a huge kitchen which seemed to be the living room as well. We had toast and honey and apple juice, and when we'd finished Rem's mum took us for a walk through parts of the big house. She didn't have white hair; she had red hair a bit like Eric's only even more of it, and very frizzy.

As we walked I decided I would call him Rem – even if he had tricked us about the tunnel. He obviously thought being called Remmy was a bit childish – like me being called Jimmy instead of Jim. That was something we had in common, anyway.

Anyway, the house was massive. Furniture everywhere covered in sheets, great big staircases, huge wooden doors and shutters on most of the windows. Rem's mother talked a lot as we went. It was like having a lesson or being on a school trip, which actually made sense, come to think of it, as she was the one who educated Rem at home. Loads of information about how old the house was, who the family were, how they ran the place, the gadgets and how it was pretty well self-sufficient with the farm, vegetable gardens and orchards. She even showed us how the servants' bells worked and how they were all connected to the kitchen where we'd had our snacks.

We talked about the lost names on the station subway wall and how most of them were killed in the First World War so never came back to work at the station, and how when the war was over there was hardly anyone left to run the house. The saddest part was about how the two sons of the family that owned the house were also killed in the war and how their mum and dad sort of lost heart after that. This house had been their big family project; they'd all been involved in its development – like the fantastic railway station and the subway with the blue tiles. I bet the sons had a hand in that. After the war – almost everyone had gone. The mum and dad didn't see the point in the house or the station. So they let the railway company close the station and the branch line, left the house to some cousins and moved away. Then the cousins left the house to someone else, or sold it, or handed it down but no-one ever really lived here again. It became like a family heirloom that you keep in a drawer. People like Rem's mum were employed to keep it in one piece but Crowton Manor never really *lived* again.

"What about Envelope the Horse? Why was he called Envelope?" said Arthur as though he'd been waiting to ask all afternoon. He probably had.

"I know the answer to that," interrupted Rem. "When the station was in full use, Envelope the Horse pulled a cart from the station up to the house with people's luggage and trunks and parcels – whatever. But – my dad told me this – this horse was useless when the driver had to back the cart up. He couldn't back up in a straight line, so the cart would go all over the place. It would like fold up and get stuck. Like an Envelope! So they called him Envelope! I think they took him to France with them for the war, which is why his name is on the list."

"Whose name is on the list?" It was a man's voice, coming from the porch way just outside the kitchen door.

They all turned to see who was coming into the room.

It was Mr Nixon!

"Hi Dad," said Rem. "These are my new friends."

"They look as though they need a good wash," he said as though he'd never seen us before in his life. "Soil everywhere."

****

12.

The interview

I hated this!

We'd only just got into our classroom on Monday morning and some kid came in with a note for us to go and see Mr Nixon. I knew what would happen. He would make us wait for hours, then he'd call us in one at a time, then he would bark to scare who was still waiting outside; then he wouldn't let us talk and all the time there would be the unspoken threat that any second he would bite your arm or your leg or your head completely off.

We were not happy, but when we got to his office, the door was slightly ajar only this time, unlike that slightly ajar door at Henley Phipps' house, we didn't dare peep through. There are some things that just can't be looked at – like an open stock room door revealing a pile of dead kids or Mr Nixon – Mr Rembrandt Nixon senior to be exact – sharpening a big knife and laughing like an evil wizard.

"Come in," said a voice that sounded almost normal: no sounding the end of the sentence twice over ('come in-na'), no barking, no irritation, just, "Come in." Don't get me wrong, I'm not saying he sounded friendly, just not absolutely disgusted that he was going to have to have a conversation with us.

"You left my house so quickly yesterday that I'm feeling there must be more to say. Certainly I have more to say, but I thought I ought to give you the chance to ask me – whatever you might want to ask me."

Eric and Arthur said, "No sir" in unison and I said, "What about, sir?" at the same time. Victor just waited.

"Anything at all, Mr McConkey. Anything at all?"

"Well I was wondering…" the others looked at me horrified thinking I was going to ask him if his first name really was Rembrandt, "…about the names on the subway wall. What's a lengthman? It said, 'Charlie Thurlwell, lengthman'. I just wondered what…erm ….."

"He had to walk along the tracks tapping them and checking the fixings. To make sure they were safe. A bit like my job in the school really, walking along the corridors tapping children on the heads and making sure they are safe."

"Oh! Right, sir."

"They puzzled you, did they, the names on the wall. That sad list of ex-railway employees?"

"We thought they were interesting, didn't we?" said Arthur nodding and looking to us hoping for support.

I started to reel off some of the names: "Charlie Thurlwell, Freddie Ditchfield, Ted Buckley...."

"Alfred Davenport," volunteered Eric.

"Exactly! It's more than a hundred years since they were all together at Crowton Halt. I think it might help if you didn't talk about them now, certainly not to Remmy – not even to each other. Say nothing. Anything else?"

What was wrong with talking about them? Weren't you supposed to talk about those people who died in the wars? We all shook our heads, tried to look innocent and turned towards the door.

"Oh yes, sir, I was wondering...." Arthur piped up and we all turned towards him, willing him to shut up so that we could leave. "I was – er – what's a postal order, sir? And tuck. What's tuck?"

"Why do you ask?" He clearly thought that Arthur had lost his mind.

"Billy Bunter and this poem about trains carrying postal orders."

"You used to be able to buy a postal order, for any value you chose, at the Post Office. Then you would send it to someone as a birthday present, for instance. They would cash it in at the Post Office and spend it. On tuck perhaps. Food. Billy Bunter was in a story-book boarding school called Greyfriars."

"Thank you sir," I said, taking Arthur by the elbow and turning towards the door. Why did he ask about postal orders? Why did he keep us there a second longer than.....the open door beckoned.

"Good. No don't leave." Mr Nixon held up an arm, like a traffic policeman. Pause. "I didn't say you could leave. I'm not going to ask why you came to my house, or why you had conversations with my son and my wife. In fact,

I'm not going to quiz you any further at all about your *intrusion* into my private life. I'm going to let it lie. I can't understand why, but my son Rembrandt would like you to visit him again..."

We all breathed out, but I don't think he noticed.

"... and I have no objection – on the strict condition that you bring no one else with you, and tell no one else about the existence of my house, Crowton Mill, Crowton Halt, Crowton Manor and most of all my family, especially my son. Got it?"

"Yes sir," we all said together.

"And you certainly don't make any reference to any long dead railway employees, even if you do know their names. See you on Saturday morning, then. No earlier than ten. You can leave now, thank you."

We left, trying not to bump into each other in our eagerness to get through the door.

You know that sort of walk-run you do down corridors at school, with your hands flat and your arms going like clockwork soldiers? We did that – until we got to our classroom. At the door I placed my hand on the handle and turned to the others. "Arthur. Postal orders? Tuck? What were you thinking of - asking Nixon questions? He's probably phoning the child psychologist now."

"I couldn't think of anything else to say."

"You could have just said nothing."

"No I couldn't. The way he looks at you, you just have to confess whatever's in your head."

Shaking our heads, we went into the classroom, just in time to see Mr Hetherington finishing off a bag of crisps and screwing up the packet.

****

13.

Friday night

Friday night was my mum and dad's night off. He didn't work late and she didn't cook. We had fish and chips from the chippy and watched a DVD, by the end of which they were both almost always asleep, which at least meant that I got to stay up much later than usual. It was funny watching them sleep because it was probably the only time they stopped talking and sat still. Salt and vinegar on your fingers, a DVD, sound turned quite low, and breathing from my mum and dad which occasionally overflowed into a snore. I liked Friday nights.

When the phone rang I quickly assumed the deep sleep position. It was like a reflex action; if you want to escape something you really do not want to face, go to sleep as fast as possible. My mother grumbled herself up from the sofa and went to the phone. Pause. Hushed voices. Then: "Jimmy! Wake up! It's for you."

"I'm asleep."

"No you're not. There's someone on the phone for you, so will you please not show me up by moaning in front of this person, who can hear every word that you say, and do as you're told!"

It was bound to be Henley Phipps asking when we were going to take him to Crowton Mill. He'd be all wheedling and smarmy; then he'd switch tack and hint at what he might do to me if I didn't get a move on making a decision about the trip; then he'd start going on about zombies and how it was probably the zombies that caused the blood clot in his head and how he was on a mission to eliminate zombies – except he wouldn't say 'eliminate'; then he would .... "Hello? It's me, Jim. Who is it?"

"Jim? It's Rem."

"Oh! Rem. Brilliant! I thought it might be somebody else. How did you get my phone number?"

"Who did you think might be phoning you from Crowton Mill?"

"No – not from there – not from Crowton – I thought it might be somebody else - someone from round where I live. This kid who's always picking on me."

"That's another thing we have in common, then isn't it, bullying."

"A bit, yeah. Well, a lot actually."

"You ought to get your mum to educate you at home."

"She'd end up killing me. I think I'd drive her mad. What did you phone me about?"

"Are you still coming tomorrow?"

"Course we are."

"That's all right then. Brilliant! Just thought I'd check – and…" he paused, "Are you still there?"

"Yeah."

"It *was* me in your garden the other week. I sneak out on my bike sometimes for a ride, when it's just going dark so no one sees me. I'd seen you and Arthur, and Eric, and Victor on the estate."

"We've never seen you."

"That's because you're always talking and laughing, you probably never see anyone except each other. No wonder someone bullies you. They're probably jealous of all the laughs you have and how you don't see anyone else."

"You should have come up and said something to us, Rem."

"You'd have run a mile. Look at me! Anyway, that's all, see you tomorrow, Jim," he said cheerfully and put the phone down.

I went and sat down in the living room. My mum and dad seemed to be asleep and the DVD was still playing, but I couldn't follow what was going on.

"That was Remmy Nixon, wasn't it?" said my mother so that I nearly jumped out of my skin.

"I thought you were asleep."

"The phone woke me up. Remember?"

"How do you know him? How do you know his name? He never goes out."

"Except sometimes he has to go to the optician's! Duhh!"

"Has he really got transparent eyes?"

"Of course they're not transparent! He has no colour pigment in his irises which makes them look as though they're transparent."

"How did you know that I knew him?"

"I know everything, James McConkey; you should know that by now. Do you really think I'd be letting you ride all over the place on your bike without checking up on where you're going? Anyway, I saw his mother at the shops."

"I think you see everybody at the shops. It's like the shops' secret service: spies pretending to be shopping and passing secret messages and watching people."

"So – I just thought I'd say – it's a good thing, making friends with Remmy. He has to stay in most of the time."

"It's Rem, actually. Remmy is a baby's name."

"Of course it is – *Jim*."

I think that was the first time ever that she'd called me Jim. I was just thinking that I must have grown up when she said, "And by the way! When are you going to do as you're told about answering that phone? You realise it woke me up, and you know very well it's Friday night, and don't tell me you were asleep as well, because I know you weren't and don't ask me how I know, I just know....I'm your mother!"

I reached for the TV control to turn the sound up but then thought better of it.

****

14.

How were we to know?

How were we to know as we rode our bikes from the five-a-day estate towards Crowton Mill on that late September Saturday morning that we were being followed? Convinced that wherever we were Nixon would be able to hear us, we had said nothing to anyone at school. We'd said hardly anything to each other! I hadn't even mentioned Rem's phone call the night before. On that Saturday morning, we were so relaxed, so pleased and so happy to be going back to the lost train station and the story-filled manor house and the kid with transparent eyes that we didn't even look over our shoulders as we rode purposefully on towards who knows what relics and wonders waiting for us at Crowton Mill?

Had we looked back, we would have seen two following bikes: one ridden by a boy wearing a balaclava and the other ridden by a boy with a head like a pea. Henley Phipps, the masked avenger and his mountainous side kick, Chucky Lockett,

We parked our bikes up near the concealed tunnel and sat down on the grass to wait for Rem. We said we'd meet him here, but I had no intention of going down that tunnel again. Sitting there looking at the entrance I could see that Rem must have burrowed through some earlier soil landslide that had probably slipped down the embankment – because of rain or just because of its own weight. It had blocked off the subway entrance and although the burrowed tunnel itself was only about three metres long the thought of that weight of soil above it, poised to slip further down, with no notice, filled me with dread. Thinking about it made one of my knees start to shake like it does when you climb a tree and realise that you're far too high and if you try to climb further up *or* down you will definitely plummet to earth. So you freeze. In terror.

"Why would anyone want to hurt Rem?" said Victor.

We all just went, "Umm."

"Why do people always have to have some other people that they hate and then go on about how we've got to stick together to sort them out, get rid of them, whatever that means – as though anyone who isn't from round here, or who talks differently…

"Or likes poems," said Arthur.

"Or various types of heavy transport," enthused Eric.

"Or has a long lost granddad name," Victor said.

"Or has a beard – or a bald head," Arthur was on a roll.

"Steady on, Arthur. You've got to draw the line somewhere," Victor laughed.

"Or people who are completely white in every detail, so they must be an alien or a zombie," I said trying to keep the list going.

"Or who are named after motor bike aces from 1907," Victor went on, "or who have dads with strange names and stranger jobs."

"Lost names, poetry, transport geeks, albinos …. sort – them –out! Send for Henley the Destroyer. Call Chucky the Hulk. They will defend you from – everything!" I said, forgetting just for a minute that terrible dark tunnel mouth just a few feet from us.

"It's so easy to hate someone when you can pick on just one thing about them, isn't it? Like white hair or a funny name. If you can think of them as just this one thing – and not have to see all the other things about them – then…..Like us and Henley. All we see in him is his sneery voice."

"And his scars," said Arthur.

"And his bossiness," added Eric.

"And his completely empty head," I said and everyone laughed.

Our laughter was interrupted by Arthur who suddenly stood up, pointed and said, "Is that a couple of blokes up at the top of the embankment?"

We all looked. Standing among the trees and undergrowth at the top of the embankment there were two men or at least the silhouettes of two men - well, two people anyway - both wearing caps and dark clothes, facing in our direction and standing very still.

Eric gasped, "They're not railway workers, are they?"

"How can they be, there's no railway here, is there," I said, suddenly feeling cold.

There was a pause - then things began to happen so fast and in so many different directions that we totally forgot about the blokes watching us from the hill.

At the far end of the mill pond, Rem appeared, and shouted to us. Before he could lower his waving arm, two other figures emerged from the muddy lane that led from the main road to the mill and they too began shouting and waving their arms. They dropped their bikes and began to run towards Rem who in turn began to run towards us. By this time we were all jumping up and down and shouting, "Run, Rem, run!" like a crowd watching a race.

As the two heaving figures came within earshot we could clearly hear Henley's voice shouting, "Zombie," and "Get him!" but then as Henley's words began to sink into his companion's brain, the lumbering figure hesitated and then stopped.

He was suddenly and very obviously afraid. He had seen what he thought was a zombie – and what's seen cannot be unseen.

We couldn't hear exactly what he was saying but there were words like 'eat' and 'face' and 'dead' and 'zombie' all mixed up with what sounded like crying coming from the very small head on top of the huge body. I don't think he said "Mummy!" but I wouldn't be surprised if he did.

Henley was shouting, and now we could hear him quite clearly, "You might as well clear off home then, you useless article. I don't know why I brought you anyway. I'm going tell everyone you blubbed when you saw the zombie. You know they call you pea head, don't you…"

Under this barrage of insults Chucky Lockett was now crying - out loud – wailing – howling that he didn't like zombies, he'd never liked zombies, his mum told him to keep away from zombies…. "Don't make me talk to the zombie, Hen. Don't make me sort him out, Hen. I'm really scared of zombies!"

All this gave us the chance to run. Rem pointed to the tunnel. I shouted, "No!" Rem shouted "Yes!" Arthur disappeared into the dark. Eric followed. Victor said, "Jim, you've got to!" I said, "No I haven't!" Rem said, "That kid with the balaclava is going to kill us all!" I said, "No he isn't!" Victor said, "See you," and disappeared into the dark. Rem said, "When are you going to do as you're told?" I said, "I hate tunnels" and crawled in. Rem followed. I could feel him behind me pushing the soles of my shoes which meant I got to the other end quite quickly really!

Silence. Breathing. Fear and exhaustion all mixed together. In the dark I had this picture of Henley stuck in my head, frozen as I'd seen him just before crawling into the tunnel, heaving himself after us with a fishing rod on his back and carrying a big heavy bag.

Rem's torch came on and took in each of our faces one at a time. "We can't stay here. He'll follow. Let's get to the house."

We didn't argue and with barely a glance at the list of names on the wall or the blue and white tiles, began climbing the stairs towards the light.

We were almost at the top when our progress was frozen by a huge and echoing roar coming from beyond the subway and echoing through the tunnel: "Youuuuu! McConkeyyyyy! Just you waitttttt!" The subway was acting like a megaphone so that Henley Phipps' voice boomed and vibrated through what was left of the railway station. It sounded more than anything like an oncoming train.

At which we ran towards the house.

****

15.

Talk to Me

When we reached the house, Rem retrieved a door key from under a plant pot and let us into the kitchen. He explained that his mother was almost certainly somewhere in one of the scores of rooms or corridors in the house cleaning or mending something and his dad was out.

"Where's he gone?" asked Arthur rather tentatively. "Will he come back any minute?"

"That's a very subtle question Arthur," Victor laughed, "give us a time, Rem, and we'll make sure we've gone before he comes in!"

"He works for the Samaritans all day Saturday once a month. It's today."

"The what?"

"They help people. They talk to them on the phone, listen to them and give them advice. If someone is having problems or is very unhappy, they can phone up for help. My dad just talks to them over the phone. Listens, and tries to make them feel a bit better."

We didn't do anything meaningful with our eyes; we just went quiet and sort of glanced at each other. I was trying to picture Mr Nixon being nice to someone but the picture just wouldn't form in my mind. He probably hissed at them – and barked – and threatened to bite them if they didn't cheer up – but then if it was on the phone, it might not be quite as bad.

Then I said, in an attempt to pre-empt anyone saying the wrong thing, "We ought to give Henley the Samaritans' number. He needs to feel a bit better." Everyone laughed.

"I can still hear him roaring," said Arthur. "Henley Phipps."

We all listened.

No, nothing. Not even dogs barking somewhere miles away.

"Was Chucky Lockett crying before, or did I dream that?" I said, again trying to lighten the mood.

"Shut up a minute! Listen!

There was definitely a voice. Distant but audible. If it was Henley, he sounded more deranged than ever. Scars all over his face, his best mate crying and wanting to run home to his mother, and his new best mates, as he thought – us – abandoning him and not bringing him to catch fish and – having to wear a balaclava! He was a soul in torment and he was not going to go away.

"You're not doing the empathy thing again are you, Jim?" said Victor. "Forget empathy just think *irrevocable*. *Unstoppable*. Sorry, Rem, Jimmy has this affliction: he keeps feeling sorry for terrible people."

"Had we better find your mum?" said Eric uncomfortably - obviously thinking like me that Rem might think Victor meant him as well.

So that was the plan. The house was so massive we all went off in different directions – believing – hoping – that

Henley Phipps wouldn't break into the house and pick us off one by one.

I thought that my best bet was to climb the nearest staircase and get as high up in the house as I could, so at least Henley's face wouldn't appear at a window – where he would whip his balaclava off, waggle his scars at me, bare his teeth and make biting movements with his mouth.

I went from room to room, all the way along the top floor. Some had posh furniture, some were just empty and one of them was a bathroom with a really old and big bath, with like green streaks leading from the tap down to the plug hole. There were loads of cast iron fittings holding up the bath, the toilet and the sink. This house was like a museum.

No sign of Rem's mum. No sound of Rem's mum. More to the point, no sign of Henley Phipps so I thought the best thing to do was sit down on the top of the stairs; listen and wait. No point in looking for trouble. I could just sit there, relax, breathe and try to imagine what this amazing house would have been like when it was full of people and there were trains puffing through the station and Envelope the Horse was getting all tied up in knots trying to back his cart up carrying the people's luggage.

The trouble was, those nice thoughts were interrupted by a memory. The time we were playing kick-the-can and I got trapped in that hedge and the darkness went all really threatening. All my friends left me on my own, being soaked up by the hedge and the night, and those faces just there – well, just nearly there. Perhaps this is what was happening now? Perhaps Victor and them had forgotten me, or couldn't find me or Henley had killed them all or – this was really bad – perhaps I'd fallen through a hole in time and was left stranded in the future or in the past – all on my own! Or perhaps I was imagining that this was a house because I was making my mind forget that I was in a tunnel and I was stuck and the roof was pressing down and there were no faces in the dark because there was nothing....nothing...

A phone rang.

I *was* in a house. It had a phone in it. In one of the bedrooms and it was ringing. Probably for me, my mother asking me when I was going to do as I was told, or – this was better - Rem's mum telling me to come down and have some toast and honey.

I ran from room to room and in the biggest room, with a big bed and tall furniture, I found this really old fashioned white phone. Alongside it, perfectly placed on the bedside table, was a note pad and a little pencil with a silver top.

For once in my life I was going to do as I was told. I picked up the phone. It was quite heavy actually. "Hello!" I said into the phone.

"Am I speaking to the big house?" a man's voice, very polite.

"Yes. Well, you're speaking to *someone* in the big house." (Stop being clever, Jim, I thought, just answer the man!) "My name is Jim."

"Oh, thank goodness! Thank you, Jim. There's been an accident at the station. It looks like some sort of roof collapse and we can hear someone in there. Would it be possible for someone at the big house to come down and give us a hand? It's a person. We think he's trapped under the station."

"Hang on, right! Okay," I said writing some words on the note pad, just as I was always told. Roof collapse; station; person trapped. "I'll go. I'll find someone. I'm going now!"

"Thank you very much, sir."

Sir? No time - I was gone, half falling down the stairs and after a few false turns into the wrong rooms I found the kitchen, where everyone, including Mr and Mrs Nixon, was standing about holding plates, waiting for the snack to be toasted.

"Ah! The lost boy," said Mr Nixon.

"There's been an accident at the station. Someone's trapped." I said running towards the back door and struggling to open it. "Come on. We've got to go."

I tumbled out into the open and ran, followed, and then overtaken, by the others. Across what used to be a garden, through the undergrowth, down the steps into the subway with Mr Nixon shouting, over and over, "Hello! Are you all right? Anybody hurt?" He had brought one of those big torches with him from the kitchen and was now shining it around the subway. The names on the wall. The tulip tiles. The tunnel.

Silence. More silence. Everyone looked at me with a 'what are you talking about' look on their faces.

"I'm stuck!" A small, pathetic little voice. Definitely Henley's, but now shrunk to the voice of a little boy.

"Remmy, run up to the house and get a spade from the shed." Remmy went. "Has the roof collapsed?" he called into the tunnel.

"I'm just stuck!"

"What's your name, son?"

"Henley Phipps, Mr Nixon."

"You? You're supposed to be at home getting better." There was a long pause. "Henley? Are you still there? Talk to me."

"I only wanted to go fishing, Mr Nixon. I can't move in here, Mr Nixon. I think the air's running out and this balaclava is all twisted round my head."

Mr Nixon shone his torch briefly into the tunnel and continued to talk calmly to Henley about pike and carp and how he would get him a permit to fish in the mill pond. At one point Henley stopped talking again and, despite Mrs Nixon's protests, Mr Nixon tried to squeeze himself into the tunnel to reach him but he was too big, so when he backed out I took the torch from his hand, and poked my head into the darkness. I think I heard Victor ask me what I was playing at, but I couldn't stand there just waiting and anyway, I think my brain, or at least my imagination, had closed down.

I wriggled into the tunnel with the torch shining ahead of me in one hand and my other hand reaching forward towards where I thought Henley might be. The balaclava was all rucked up over one of his eyes and his gaping mouth was just showing beneath. I don't think I'd ever seen it not sneering before.

"Henley it's me, can you grab my hand?"

"Who's me?" he said.

"Jim. It's Jimmy McConkey."

"Bog off, McConkey. I'm not being rescued by you, Jimmy McConkey. You left me behind – after all I've done for you. You said you'd come fishing with me and I was really looking forward to it! Now I'll probably die in this hole and it'll all be your fault."

I think he was crying but it wouldn't have been the right time to point this out to him, or anybody else. So I just reached forward and grabbed his sleeve.

"Get your hands off me, McConkey," he said, flapping his hands like you do at a wasp, but I held on.

As best I could, I shouted back over my shoulder for Mr Nixon to pull me out by my ankles while I held onto Henley. In the end, after moving him only about half a metre, I had to let go of Henley's sleeve and allow myself to be pulled out of the tunnel, falling onto the ground just as Rem arrived with the spade. Victor, Arthur and Eric were looking at me. I'm not sure if their faces were trying to signal horror or disgust. Arthur mouthed the word, "What?" at me and turned the palms of his hands up towards the ceiling.

Mr Nixon dug away at the tunnel in an attempt to create a much bigger space. After several thuds of soil onto the subway floor, a lot of grunting and heavy breathing, there was a clank. Metal on metal. The spade had hit something.

"Has he hit Henley's head?" said Arthur.

"What on earth...?" Mr Nixon fell to his hands and knees and reached into the tunnel. More heavy breathing and strained grunting, then in a shower of earth Mr Nixon's pulled from the tunnel a huge white metal plate with 'Beware of the Trains: By Order' written on it in raised black letters.

From the darkness came a strangled wail: "Don't let McConkey and them have it, Mr Nixon. It's mine!"

Mr Nixon fell to his knees again, did a bit more digging, reached forward, grabbed Henley by the back of his shirt and pulled. It was like when a calf or a lamb is born. Henley slithered out face down and crumpled, coughing and spitting, to the floor. As he staggered to his feet he was wrestling with his balaclava so that he could see what was happening. It finally came off, in a shower of soil, revealing his flame red scars. Mrs Nixon gasped.

Victor stepped forward reassuringly, "It's all right, Mrs Nixon. His head was like that before."

"Let's get everyone up to the house," said Mrs Nixon. She said to Henley, "Can you walk?" She hadn't heard his name properly, so didn't know what to call him.

Mr Nixon took Henley's arm and half lifted, half led him up the subway steps. As they made their way towards the house, Henley looked back at me over his shoulder. "Don't you tell people you rescued me, McConkey, because you didn't! It was Nixon what rescued me – sorry sir, Mr Nixon. Sorry sir, I didn't think. Have you still got my balaclava? Where's my Beware of the Trains sign?"

"I've got your balaclava," said Rem and handed it to Henley – who looked suspiciously at Rem, then at the balaclava and then snatched it. "I'll carry the trains notice if you like," Rem offered helpfully.

Henley just grabbed the big cast iron notice and although it was too heavy to carry comfortably put it under his arm and walked awkwardly towards the house. "And you needn't think you're getting this, McConkey, because you're not."

As they walked on Henley twisted himself round, nodded towards Rem and said to Mr Nixon. "That's that zombie, isn't it sir? Have you captured him?" Mr Nixon didn't reply, just gripped Henley more tightly under the arm, half lifting him off the ground, and marched him more quickly towards the house – with Henley saying, "Ow, ow, ow, sir, ow," all the way along the path.

I slowed down and let them go on ahead of me. No-one even said one word about how brave *I'd* been, how I'd overcome, just for a few minutes, my absolute terror of small places and the dark. Typical! Just wait till one of you lot wants rescuing, I thought, don't come running to me.

****

16.

Sir

Back at the house, it was all go. Henley was sent into the bathroom to attempt a quick wash and to refit his balaclava, Mrs Nixon made toast and Mr Nixon phoned Henley's mother and a taxi to pick her up, bring her to the house and then take them back home or to hospital, whatever she thought best.

When he returned to the kitchen he plonked himself in a chair and glared sulkily at us all. Mr Nixon approached, gently lifted him by his shoulders from the chair and began to straighten his clothes. Henley stood up very straight and still and his eyes got bigger and bigger as if he was expecting something frightening or painful to happen. Then just as carefully, Mr Nixon took Henley's shoulders and sat him down. Henley did a look to us that said, "See, I wasn't scared. I don't get scared, me," but of course made no sound.

"This iron notice, Henley: Beware of the Trains. By order. Where did you get it?"

"I found it, sir, in the woods by the pond," Henley said, proudly.

"Then it belongs here, doesn't it. I think I'll bury it with the station. What do you think, Henley?"

"Finders keepers I thought, sir," said Henley.

"I knew you'd understand, Henley."

"Do I?" said Henley puzzled, then, as though he had suddenly received a secret and that none of us could possibly appreciate what he and Mr Nixon knew, he said, "Oh yeah, I get it, yes sir. I understand. Bury it, with the station. What station?"

Mr Nixon said nothing, just winked. As a result Henley looked very pleased with himself and kept smiling and nodding at Mr Nixon and giving him the thumbs-up sign.

When the taxi arrived with Henley's mum there were various explanations, thanks, reassurances and goodbyes. As they were leaving, Mr Nixon put his arm around Henley's shoulder and nodded towards Rembrandt. "That kid there, Henley. That's my son. His name is Rembrandt and he's not a zombie."

Henley looked, thought about it, and sneered a Henley sneer. "You're having me on, sir, no one's called Rembrandt."

"It's a family name after the TT rider and it's my name too. We're both called Rembrandt," said Mr Nixon.

"That's nice isn't it, Henley?" said Mrs Phipps, "It's nice when you have a family name, isn't it? An unusual name and all, isn't it, Henley. Well, come on then, say thank you to everyone, Henley, we'll get you off to the hospital."

"Mm!" said Henley and he got into the taxi he said, "Ow, ow, ow!" again and put his hand over his scars as though in terrible pain, but as it drove off he swivelled his head in the balaclava and looked at me through the side window of the taxi and did that thing people do - pointing at himself then at me several times, very fast – with a fierce look on his face. Then he saw Mr Nixon watching him so he smiled a twisted smile and put his thumbs up.

For a moment Eric, Arthur, Victor, Rem, Mr Nixon, Mrs Nixon and I just stood there watching in silence as the taxi bumped along the muddy lane towards the main road.

"A close shave," said Mr Nixon. "He really could have suffocated in that tunnel, you know. I'm filling it in after tea, Remmy, burying all of it, including that Beware of the Trains notice. It needs to be back where it belongs with the station and the names on the wall. And I think you'd better give the station remains a bit of a wide berth for the foreseeable future – all of you – I just want to bury the dead, not the living, whatever you think I do to people I don't approve of!! It all needs checking. But – having said that, I have to say to you lot, well done! You were very helpful – especially you, James, alerting us like that. What? Did you hear something or see something? How did you know he was trapped?"

"The man on the telephone told me." Long pause. Mr and Mrs Nixon just stared at me so I added, "In one of the top bedrooms. My mum's always going on at me and telling me I've got to answer the phone, so I answered it."

I couldn't make out if they were cross or concerned. They just said, "Which room? Come on, show us," so we all traipsed up the stairs to the bedroom where I'd answered the phone. No-one spoke just half ran up the stairs to this bedroom with me thinking was I going to get the telling- off of my life. About what I didn't know, but most of the time I get told off I don't know what I've done – until I'm told off about it, of course.

There was no phone on the bedside table. I looked at everyone.

Eric and Arthur had that 'don't involve me' look on their faces; Victor and Rem were deadly serious.

"There's no phone in here," said Mr Nixon. "In fact, there're no landline, or fixed, phones in the whole house, haven't been for years. So what are you talking about?"

With a rising feeling of panic I went across to the bedside table and saw a notepad and a little silver pencil. On the note pad was written: 'Roof collapse; station; person trapped'. I held it out to Mr Nixon and said, "It was a big white phone and a man spoke to me – and he called me, 'sir'."

****

17.

Full stops and stories

It's funny but hardly any of this ever got mentioned again. I suppose, because - what can you say? It's like that saying, 'sentences have full stops, but stories don't.' There was no way to finally explain what had happened except to say, Henley lived, his scars faded and changed but his character stayed the same; Rem kept on being educated at home but slowly began to be seen on the estate and at the shops; Mr Nixon was still the deputy head at our school but for some reason we hardly ever saw him and the lost names gang kept on finding and going on and on about whatever enthusiasm came up next – as long as there was a poem in it for Arthur to learn and shout out from his bike, an engine to marvel at for Eric and a rights and wrongs debate for Victor to challenge us with.

At home, my mother kept on finding reasons to say, 'When are you going to do as you're told?' and 'Where did you learn language like that?' whenever I repeated a word she thought was a swear word and had just used.

And I answered the phone at home, whenever it rang, but it was never that man again or any of those men who left Crowton Halt station to go off to the war with most of them never coming back. They probably called themselves 'The Crowton Pals' as they wrote the date and their names on the subway wall:

October 1914
Stanley Greenhouse, booking clerk
Freddie Ditchfield, porter
Charlie Thurlwell, lengthman.
Phineas George Hewitt, guard.
Alfred Davenport, signalman.
Ted Buckley, footplate.
Len Hodgkinson, driver.
Percy Rembrandt Nixon, station foreman.
Envelope the horse

Except they did come back, didn't they? Maybe, despite everything that happened to them, they never really left. I know I believe that, and I'm certain there are other people who do too.

****

Thanks

Enormous thanks go to my wife Chris for her support, patience and uncompromising proof reading; to actor Tony Turner and screenwriter Roy Mitchell, my irreplaceable critical friends; to Derryck Cox for all his advice on long forgotten railway stations; to the children of Class 6 at Lightwoods Primary School, for their hugely helpful reading of the story's first draft, and to their teacher, Charlotte Hankin who supported their involvement so unstintingly.

Acknowledgements

The poem that Arthur loves and keeps quoting is: 'Night Train' by W.H. Auden.

The story of Envelope the Horse is told by Bob Downes in a collection of railway memories called, *Stories of the Somerset and Dorset* by Alan Hammond: Millstream Books 1995

03456 024348.

Lightning Source UK Ltd.
Milton Keynes UK
UKOW04f1238121214

243045UK00001B/104/P